MULLED WINE AND MURDER

A CHARLETON HOUSE MYSTERY

KATE P ADAMS

Cover design by Dar Albert

To
Julian and Lenny Kiss.
Angus, Finlay and Tom McCormack.

Young men who give me hope for the future.

CHAPTER 1

I was slowly and carefully laying a delicate piece of gold leaf onto a plain wooden photo frame. It was a challenge to stop it splitting, or creasing on top of itself and forming raised gold veins on the wood as I gave it a gentle brush with the soft bristles of what I'd learnt was called a 'gilder's mop'.

When one of the Charleton House conservation team had offered to run a gilding workshop on a Sunday afternoon to give staff the chance to make some very special Christmas gifts, I had eagerly signed up. Now I was intensely focused, trying to make the frame as beautiful as possible and deciding who would find it under their Christmas tree.

'Sophie... Sophie... Sophie! Look.' I'd forgotten that Mark Boxer, my friend and a tour guide at Charleton House, was beside me, a sure sign of how hard I was concentrating. I glanced over at his grinning face.

'How do I look? I reckon this will do for the Christmas party.' Mark, who was known for giving engaging, fascinating tours to royalty, political dignitaries and both major and minor celebrities, was smiling from beneath a gilded moustache.

'Is that what you've spent the last half hour doing?' I asked wearily.

'Yeah – great, eh!'

I knew this wasn't a question. His perfectly shaped handlebar moustache now glinted in the light and looked like a carved piece of solid gold. I was trying to decide whether it was modern art worthy of a place in the Duke and Duchess of Ravensbury's art collection or a shiny slug that had neglected to read the dress code.

'I'd make a great Christmas decoration.'

'In a house of horrors,' boomed the unmistakable dulcet tones of Joyce Brocklehurst over my shoulder. 'Have you any idea how much that stuff costs?'

'Spoilsport,' he fired back. 'I think it looks rather magnificent. Seriously though, shall I keep it like this for tonight?'

'Not if you ever want to be taken seriously again,' I advised. 'Save that sort of thing for outside work. Maybe Bill would appreciate it.' I wondered if Mark's husband would react any differently to Joyce and me. Mark seemed to be thinking about it.

'That's not a bad idea. I'll be the gilded gift under the tree that awaits him on Christmas morn. That or I'll be the fairy on the top of the tree.' He guffawed at his own joke. Joyce and I rolled our eyes at one another and started to pack up. The class was over and we needed to don our glad rags for the Charleton House staff Christmas party.

The Gilded Hall could have been an appropriate place for Mark to reveal his newly styled moustache, but I also liked the idea of him having his reputation remain intact, so I was pleased that he had removed the gold leaf before joining the staff party. The large, grandly decorated hall with an imposing staircase at the centre was full of happy staff. Light from faux candles and twinkling Christmas lights danced along the walls. The gilded balcony railing, after which the room was named, glowed warmly. The figures in the baroque fresco that covered the ceiling watched the revellers below as they laughed, drank champagne, caught up with colleagues from different departments, and no doubt gossiped as the wine loosened tongues.

The Duke and Duchess of Ravensbury, whose family had owned Charleton House since it had been built in 1550, were happy to welcome the paying public in through the doors all year round. Tonight, however, they were pouring champagne for the staff. The party was their chance to thank us for all our hard work over the year, and they took that role seriously. I'd watched in amazement the first year I'd attended this event as they had worked tirelessly with the caterers who had been brought in so that my own staff could relax with everyone else. As the Head of Catering for the house, I had been both grateful and deeply impressed. I'd also found plenty of ways to help out when the Duke and Duchess weren't looking, clearing glasses and mopping up spillages.

It was still over two weeks until Christmas Day, which was fine by me as it meant I wasn't too exhausted to enjoy the evening. A huge Christmas tree stood between the bottom of the staircase and an ornate fireplace, which had been filled with beautifully decorated gifts. The fireplace itself was so big, I could stand upright in it and be fully visible. Not actually quite so impressive, being as I am barely five foot tall. The decorations on the tree were little re-creations of the 'Twelve Days of Christmas': miniature drummer boys, turtle doves, partridges. I ran through the song as I looked for all twelve designs.

This evening was a chance for the staff to have the house to themselves. They could explore the rooms without having to respond to visitors' questions or worry about whether they would get delayed on the way to a meeting. Instead, they'd admire the paintings to a soundtrack of festive tunes, listen to

Charles Dickens give a reading from *A Christmas Carol*, and then dance the night away at a party in the Garden Café.

Joyce, the retail manager for all of the gift shops, had a glass of champagne in each hand. A couple of reindeers were hanging from her ears and she wore an extremely tight low-cut red dress. The brown belt and suede wedge shoes perfectly matched the shade of the reindeers' fur, and I just hoped Rudolph hadn't been sacrificed at the altar of the perfect accessory. Joyce was somewhere the other side of sixty, we weren't sure how far, but had the body of someone less than half her age.

'Oh, don't look now,' she muttered conspiratorially.

'Since when has that phrase actually prevented anyone from looking? What have you seen?'

'It's *who* I've seen. Joe has arrived, and he's not alone.'

Detective Constable Joe Greene was a good friend, and for some time there had been an assumption that we'd end up a couple – an assumption both Joe and I had also held for a while. But I'd eventually realised it would be too much like dating a brother and let the whole idea go. I'd heard that he'd started dating Ellie Bryant, a member of the conservation team, and despite this being a staff party, no one would have stopped him coming along.

I turned my head slightly to get a surreptitious look at him. He appeared happy and relaxed in jeans and a blazer, his shirt open at the neck. His hair, which I'd never known him to pay any attention to before, looked newly trimmed and no longer fell into his eyes.

Joyce had also been assessing the new arrivals.

'You've got to give it to him, she's pretty.'

'What are you saying?' I helped myself to one of the glasses she was holding and took a drink. 'You're not getting this back now.'

'So are you!' she exclaimed. 'She's just…'

'Younger, slimmer, and has less grey hair.'

'Stop it! You look fabulous, darling. Especially now you're following my advice and adding a little colour to your funereal wardrobe.' My turquoise blouse was probably made of more fabric than Joyce's dress, and I had to admit to buying it in an attempt to get her approval. 'You could do with...' She leant towards me and with one hand undid a button. 'There, you need to show off a bit more cleavage.'

I swatted her away. 'Do you mind? Undressing me in public!' I turned to examine the damage in a large oval mirror behind me. I could barely see the top of my head.

'You look fine,' Joyce insisted, deciding the matter for me. 'Right, I need to replace the glass you stole, and mingle. My audience awaits.'

I watched as Joyce cut a path to the drinks table, and then I scanned the crowd. It was wonderful to see that Chelsea, one of my café assistants, had been able to come. She spent most of her time outside work caring for her father who had multiple sclerosis, but tonight she was able to let her hair down.

I handed my empty glass to a server as they walked past me and went to look around the rest of the house. Charleton House is a magnificent display of glittering grandeur that was built to impress. Whether you're enchanted by the view of the vast baroque palace as you drive through the estate or dazzled by its sumptuous interior, it is a building that never fails to make an impression. Its grounds are equally spectacular and its well-tended gardens a picturesque showpiece with inventive designs and surprises round every corner.

I wandered through to the music room, where the display of three beautiful harpsichords was framed by paintings by Jacopo Tintoretto, a favourite artist of one of the earlier Dukes. It was a dark room, but that simply created an atmospheric backdrop for the twinkling Christmas lights that were dotted throughout garlands running along the edges of the tables at the sides of the room. Every half hour Charles Dickens – or rather Conrad, the live interpreter who was playing him – would read to the small crowd that had gathered expectantly. The only music was Dickens's voice as it rose and fell, telling the story of Scrooge and Tiny Tim.

As I left the room, Conrad strode past me. He winked at me, acknowledged the small crowd with a smile and announced that he would start in a few moments. I'd seen many of his performances so didn't remain.

Each room on the public route held a Christmas tree, and 60,000 decorations and a million fairy lights made the house sparkle and the Christmas spirit dance among our paying visitors. I admired a collection of oriental porcelain that I hadn't noticed before displayed along a mantelpiece. The sound of carols that had gradually got louder as I'd walked through the rooms became crisp and clear as I entered onto a large landing at the top of an imposing ornate staircase. Six carol singers in Victorian dress were singing 'Ding Dong Merrily on High' and encouraging their audience to join in. I watched as our health and safety manager performed a magnificent baritone and a member of the finance department slaughtered the higher notes. Everyone was enjoying themselves and I felt like Christmas was finally here.

I strode through the last few rooms and into the Garden Café. This was the safest room to throw a slightly more rowdy party, rather than putting the house at risk, although a certain standard of behaviour was still expected and our security officers were well versed in 'helping' drunk party guests out of the building. It had previously been an orangery, and when it was built in the 1700s, it had been heated with stoves so delicate plants could be housed here during the winter months.

Now that it was an elegant café where visitors came for afternoon tea and a glass of champagne, it was perfect for events.

Here spilt drinks couldn't do permanent damage to the modern flooring, which could also handle being danced on. The white walls were the ideal backdrop for multicoloured disco lighting and the enormous floor-to-ceiling windows would reflect the festive frivolities and happy faces. The patio doors gave easy access to fresh air, and outside a corner had been set aside, with sand buckets, for smokers.

I acknowledged Briony, the caterers' manager, and walked towards her. We'd worked together a couple of times.

'Sophie, enjoying the party? It must be nice to just be a guest for a change.' She was tying her hair up and putting it in a bun as she spoke.

'Yes. I don't have to worry about running out of food, or whether my staff are late.'

'Come off it! You're like me, you can't switch off. I bet you've already cleared up dozens of glasses, watched with your heart in your mouth as someone's got a bit close to a painting or almost walked into a vase.'

I laughed – she was spot on. It was the same when I went to museums or stately homes as a visitor. I'd spot staff chewing gum or see signage that was tatty and out of date and I'd want to step in and do something about it.

'Want a quick taste of the canapés? We're just laying them out. I reckon we have fifteen minutes before people start to arrive and things get noisy.'

I followed her into an adjoining kitchen just as the main lights were switched off and we were plunged into a gold-and-pink glow. Before me was tray after tray of mouth-watering bite-sized food.

Briony talked me through them. 'We have chilli-and-marmalade glazed pork belly squares, croquettes with black pudding and apple sauce, baby sausage rolls made with turkey and cranberry. These are fidgety pies.' I bit into one of the little pies, a perfect miniature of the Derbyshire classic made with potatoes, apple, bacon, sultanas and onions, and gave her a thumbs up as I chewed. 'Our nods to dessert are mini plum puddings—' they were the size of ping-pong balls and utterly adorable '—trifle in a shot glass and little chocolate Yule logs.'

Before I knew it, I'd eaten one of each.

'They're all perfect, everyone's going to love them.'

'Good! We've made plenty as I figured there'd be a few who didn't fit in dinner before they came and might need to line their stomachs.'

We were both startled as the music started, which meant that some of the staff had made it through the house and were ready to party. I was reluctant to leave behind the food; I could have happily munched my way through an entire tray of fidgety pies, but the thought of watching some of my colleagues attempt to dance was far too tempting.

It was time to head out for some entertainment at other people's expense.

CHAPTER 2

I checked my watch: 10 pm. I'd filled up on canapés, given my best impression of dancing a couple of times and done the rounds of my team to wish them all a happy Christmas. I'd plied one of the finance managers with drink and eventually been forgiven for messing up a couple of invoices, and admired the head of security's dance moves in the hope he'd let me off losing my staff pass for a third time when I told him in the morning.

I watched as Joyce strutted her stuff on the dance floor. Mark and I sometimes joked that she was older than God, but she could dance like she was a teenager and was clearly loving every minute. As her dress slowly shuffled up, I got an eyeful of her legs, which also looked like those of an eighteen-year-old. Her mother had been a Tiller Girl, and Joyce appeared to have inherited her dancer's physique. Wisps of blonde hair were starting to release themselves from the mass that must have taken a canister of hairspray to maintain its statue-like rigidity for so long. She spun and strutted, swayed and shimmied. My feet were sore just watching her.

The last time I'd seen Mark, he'd been performing a flamboyant tango with a gardener, striding and twirling the length of the room, the two men finishing in a dramatic embrace that resulted in applause and laughter. I was considering taking my shoes off when Mark appeared beside me.

'I'm done,' I told him. 'I'm too old for this – fancy going to the Black Swan and ending our night like an old couple in the corner of the pub?'

'Are you kidding? I've only just started; I'm full of beans, pep, vigour. My body is a live wire...' He looked at me and his face crumpled into a pained expression as he continued, 'I'm exhausted, my feet hurt, I can't take it anymore.' He let his head fall onto my shoulder and cried into my ear, 'I'm soooooo old.'

I patted him on the back. 'Come on, old man, I'll settle you in next to the fire, get you a pint of stout and ask the landlord if he has a pipe and pair of slippers you can borrow.'

'Thank you,' he moaned pathetically. We left Joyce commanding the dance floor and looking like she could keep going all night. Whatever she was on, I wanted some of it.

The Black Swan pub glowed in the night. A string of lights stretched across the honey-coloured front of the 18th century building and a Christmas tree stood on either side of the door. We were wrapped in the warmth of the log fire as soon as we walked in, the low ceilings and wooden beams decorated with branches of evergreen adding to the embrace. Three more Christmas trees were dotted about the room, each decorated with red and gold baubles, miniature pint pots and silver stars. The fairies on the top were teddy bears in tutus.

As it was a Sunday night, the pub wasn't too busy, the low-level hum of conversation comforting rather than deafening. I settled Mark in at our favourite table next to the fire and went to buy our drinks.

'Isn't it your staff party?' asked Steve Seddon, the landlord.

I nodded. 'We need a sit down and a drink, we're feeling our age.'

He laughed. 'Give over, you're still a young thing. I'll bring them over – what are you having?'

'You know what we like, we'll trust you.' I turned to leave and spotted an unfamiliar face at the bar. Sitting alone at the far end was an elderly man with a flat cap and well-worn tweed jacket, his white shirt starting to show through the elbows. He smiled at me through his straggly white beard and moustache. I couldn't help but smile back; the way his eyes crinkled and shone with warmth made me think of a slightly down-at-heel Santa Claus.

Back at the table, Mark was flipping beer mats. I sat down and stared zombie-like into the fire.

'Penny for your thoughts,' said Mark.

'I was trying to remember if I've got a clean suit for work tomorrow.'

'How dull, you really are middle-aged. Shouldn't we be planning scuba diving trips, learning a new language or trekking through Mexico, trying to find the perfect coffee bean? That would be right up your street.'

I looked at him through tired eyes. 'I'd pay to see you trek to the supermarket, and you'd have an underwater panic attack if a goldfish got too close.'

'Who had a panic attack?' Steve had arrived with our drinks. 'What've I missed? Here you go, one gin and tonic – I decided you should try this one, apparently it's got notes of frankincense and myrrh in it – and, Mark, you have a pint of Dancing Elf, brewed with ginger and orange peel. They should get you in the festive mood if you're not already. Can I get you any food?'

We shook our heads simultaneously.

'Join us,' offered Mark, 'you look as tired as I feel.'

Steve plonked himself in a chair; he clearly didn't need asking twice.

'Don't mind if I do,' he said before turning towards the bar and whistling to get a member of staff's attention and miming the international signal for a drink. 'Rosemary's at her mum's, they're spending the next couple of days doing the Christmas shopping. I don't mind, she deserves a break.' Rosemary, Steve's wife, made the best sticky toffee pudding I had ever tasted; it was one of the reasons I could increasingly be described as 'curvy' at best. 'I'm also one down – one of the lads called in sick, so it's been a bit of a crazy day. Lunchtime was a challenge – I need to change over some barrels, and I still haven't put one of my deliveries in the cellar. It's been sat out the back since Friday. It'll be a late night for me.'

'You'll be alright after a good night's sleep,' offered Mark.

'Unlikely to 'appen. I never sleep well when Rosemary's away, and there's been some strange banging about going on. I think it might be the water pipes, but I can't figure out what the problem is. I haven't slept through for the last couple of days.'

'Who's the old guy?' I asked, looking in the direction of the man with the white beard. Steve wiped some beer foam off his top lip and turned to look.

'Oh, 'im. No idea. He started coming in about a week ago, seems nice enough. I'll get some mince pies brought over.' Steve stood up, steadying himself on the table as he rose. His t-shirt stretched over his large stomach as he finished his half pint. 'That'll see me to closing.'

Mark and I spent the next half hour debating which of our colleagues would phone in sick the next day as they nursed hangovers, and what ill-advised couplings we'd hear about. Neither of us were beyond a bit of good-humoured gossiping. We nibbled our mince pies politely, already sick of them having been indulging ourselves on them since mid-November, and then said goodnight.

Mark was picked up by a taxi and I wandered over the road where my home nestled in amongst a row of workers' cottages. It was appropriate, really. The original tenants would have been workers on the Charleton House estate, and now it was where I, a modern-day estate worker, lived. Although I doubted that many of the estate workers of the past were greeted by a grumpy tabby cat and a dead mouse. Such was life with a feline mistress.

After laying the mouse to rest over the garden wall, feigning pride at Pumpkin's achievement, and then pulling on my tartan flannel pyjamas, I was ready to sprawl in front of the TV. I needed half an hour to myself before going to bed.

I flicked through the channels, eventually settling on an old episode of *Miss Marple*, featuring an actress who always reminded me of my grandmother. I called Pumpkin, and in an unusual display of acquiescence, she obeyed, jumped up and stood on my chest. After my numerous attempts to get her to stop blocking my view, she chose her preferred position and lay down with her bottom inches from my face. I could hardly argue as she was facing the TV, which made a lot of sense.

I watched Miss Marple root out her clues and put an entire police department to shame, but I never got to see 'whodunit' as I fell asleep before the spinster detective had her first change of hats.

Joyce was dressed in full flamenco gear and doing a solo tango around the Charleton House visitors' car park, cheered on by the Duke who appeared to be shepherding a herd of reindeer towards the Stables Café. Joyce came to a sudden stop and started swirling her skirts around her, stamping her feet and clicking her castanets with a terrifyingly intense look in her eyes.

I woke with a start as Pumpkin launched herself off me and thudded onto the floor with the weight of a small child behind her. The sound of stamping continued and I closed my eyes, expecting to picture Joyce as she continued her routine. Nothing. Joyce had exited stage left from my imagination.

The stamping started up again. Only this time accompanied by a male voice.

'Sophie, Sophie, are you up?'

I checked my phone: it had just gone 1am. I swung my legs off the sofa and sat up. Very slowly, I stood, emitting the kind of groaning noise I'd promised myself I wouldn't make until I was ninety. The knocking was coming from my front door, but instead of a Carmen-inspired Joyce behind it, I flung it open to find a very red-faced Steve.

'Sophie, thank God! Can you come over? I've found a skeleton in the cellar.'

CHAPTER 3

*S*teve and I stood side by side, looking at a pile of rubble in the corner of the cellar.

'Over there, can you see it?'

'I can't see anything, pass me the torch. What were you doing?' I shone the torch over the stones and bricks. One did seem to be more rounded than the others; I assumed it was the skull he'd told me about.

'I needed to make room for more stock in the run-up to Christmas and I wanted to put in another set of shelves. I don't need to worry about waking Rosemary if I go to bed late, so I figured I'd just crack on and put the shelves up tonight. I was starting to move some of the stones and rubble in the corner so I could push the shelves as far back as possible and found that. There's more bones behind it.'

'When are the police arriving?'

'I haven't called them yet.'

'What? What do you mean? Call them, Steve. Why haven't you called them?'

'I don't know, I wasn't thinking. I know you've dealt with this sort of thing before and would know what to do.'

He was partly right: I had managed to get involved with a couple of murder investigations, but I certainly didn't rank above the boys and girls in blue.

'Call the police, that's what you do. Come on.' I led him back up the wooden steps to the bar where I'd be able to get a signal, and handed him my phone. With a shaky hand, Steve dialled. As he spoke to an operator, I poured him a glass of whisky. I had no idea if he liked the stuff, but it felt like something you were meant to do. He hung up and stared at the trap door.

'Thank goodness Rosemary's not here, she'd have had a fit...' He tailed off and knocked back the entire glass of whisky. I poured him more and sat him by the fire, where the embers were still glowing and it was warm and comforting.

We sat in silence for a little while until we heard the sound of a car pull up on the gravel outside, followed by the slamming of doors. Steve went over to the front door and drew back a couple of big, heavy bolts.

'Evening, Steve, I believe you've got a customer who won't leave.' DC Joe Greene grinned. 'Show us the way.'

I stepped out of the shadows and took him by surprise.

'Bloody hell, Soph, you nearly scared the... nice outfit. Looks cosy.' I was still in my tartan pyjamas. 'Going to dance the Highland Fling for us?'

'How about you go and question our friend downstairs? Will you be alright, Steve?'

'Yes, thanks. Sorry I dragged you out of bed.'

Joe was still grinning at my outfit as I left. I told myself his new girlfriend didn't wear anything quite so sexy, she was probably a flannelette nightie girl. Thank goodness the pub had been too dark for him to see what was on my feet: reindeer slippers with 3D antlers were hardly the height of fashion, but they were warm and festive and that was all that mattered.

'Nice shoes. I guess you're not vegetarian, then?' I hadn't heard a second car pull up, but I could hear the smirk in the female voice. Detective Sergeant Colette Harnby, a lopsided smile on her face, was looking like she was fighting back laughter as she assessed my choice of footwear.

'Rudolph and I need to go to bed,' I muttered.

'Sweet dreams,' she called over her shoulder as I shuffled across the road. This time I was going straight to bed, and staying there until Pumpkin decided it was time for breakfast.

I stared into my mug of coffee, watching the milk swirl into oblivion as I stirred it. I'd often wondered where I'd run and hide if zombies attacked Charleton House, but I hadn't considered my options if I became one. Today, I was definitely one of their number. As I'd stumbled my way around my own home earlier this morning, I'd stood on Pumpkin's tail, spilt coffee beans all over the floor and burnt my tongue as I drank a shot of espresso far too quickly. Worryingly, I couldn't recall my drive into work.

I now sat opposite Mark at a table in the Library Café, the book-covered walls, brown-leather armchairs and mismatched wooden furniture creating a calming atmosphere that was exactly what I needed right now. My eyes ran across the rows upon rows of hard-backed books; they would have looked at home in the Duke's own private library. In fact, he'd been involved in designing the overall theme and had wanted the book titles to reflect his family's interests and history, despite them being purely for display purposes.

My eyes were still meandering along the spines looking for titles I recognised when Mark pulled me from my dazed state.

'Are they working yet?' he asked impatiently.

'What?'

'Your jumping beans, your energy pills, those little brown oval things you're obsessed by. Coffee, woman, coffee. Wake up! It's Monday morning, get lively. I want to hear everything and that can't happen while you're practically snoring into your morning brew. At this rate, I'm going to need to perform CPR on you.'

'This might help – it'll be quicker and you won't need to have Mark's lips on you.' Chelsea had appeared as if by magic and placed an espresso in front of me. 'By the time you've finished that, your drip coffee will be cool enough to drink.'

My young assistant looked annoyingly fresh and alert. I laughed, and kept laughing. My staff knew me so well; it was both a very sweet gesture and an amusing one.

I was still laughing as Chelsea began taking all the chairs down off the tables. Already feeling perkier, I was able to fill Mark in on my early morning adventures. He sat there wide-eyed as I talked. Once I'd finished, he slowly took a drink of coffee, thought for a moment, and then spoke.

'You wore your slippers to the pub?'

I threw my head back. 'Is that what stands out for you amongst everything I've said? Yes, I wore my slippers. I was in a rush, but there was also a skeleton in the cellar, or did you miss that significant bit of information?'

'I heard you, but they're reindeer slippers and you wore them to the pub.'

'You did what?' I hadn't heard Joyce come in; she sounded horrified.

'Nothing,' I chimed loudly. Shiny Christmas presents hung from each of Joyce's ears, her emerald-green nail polish matching the wrapping.

'Wasn't it a fun night?' she declared. 'Chelsea!' she shouted across the café. 'Would you be a dear and fetch me a coffee? I need something to sharpen up the edges. Thank you.'

'Thank you?' I exclaimed. Where were Joyce's usual snapping fingers and growled demands?

'Of course, it's only polite.'

Mark and I stared at each other wide-eyed. It seemed the season of goodwill had taken root in Joyce.

She fixed her eyes on me. 'I know you like the ruffled look, but have you done *anything* with your hair this morning?' Perhaps the goodwill roots weren't firmly fixed in place yet. I ruffled my hair further just to irritate her. My messy windswept look was the most intentional part of my so-called beauty routine, and she knew that. 'Rumour has it you spent some of last night with a much older man.' She eyed me suspiciously. 'So much older, he was all bone.' Mark chuckled. 'Are you on the trail of another killer?'

'We don't know anything about him yet, and he could be a she. Joe messaged me this morning: Harnby knows the forensic pathologist really well, so he thinks she might pull in a few favours and they should be able to turn the results around pretty quickly.'

'It's going to be fascinating,' said Mark. 'This is going to be a whole different kind of investigation – we can combine your sherlocking skills, Sophie, with my research methods, and I reckon we'll know who they are by the end of the week. I bet you a chocolate croissant.'

'That all sounds rather dull,' muttered Joyce. 'I much prefer it when a bit of action is required.' She had taken to using physical persuasion when we'd found ourselves caught up in a couple of previous murder investigations.

'You can take any pent-up energy out on particularly annoying customers,' suggested Mark. 'I'm sure you've thought about it before.'

'All the time,' Joyce agreed.

'I am curious,' I admitted. 'The skeleton must have been down there long enough for business to go on for years without anyone seeing it. It was well hidden under a pile of rubble that Steve had started to clear out of the way, so I reckon it had been hidden on purpose. It wasn't an accident, but no one realised the person was missing, or didn't know where to look. Once we know how old it is, we can start looking for missing people.'

'I think the police can do that bit without our help,' said Mark. 'It might be a quick and easy job and we won't have a chance to get involved in it at all.'

'Oh, I doubt that,' said Joyce. 'Life got a lot more interesting round here after Sophie joined us and I don't think that's going to change any time soon. I can feel it in my bones. Get it? In my bones... Oh, stuff the pair of you, I thought that was rather good.'

She got up and made for the door. I looked over at Mark and was certain he was thinking the same as me. Hopefully the police wouldn't have an easy job, we both loved a good mystery.

CHAPTER 4

*A*fter Mark and I had topped up our caffeine levels we'd moved on to sugar, and after a couple of chocolate croissants, I was ready to start my day. My first stop was a visit to the Charleton House chapel. Christmas was one of the few times of the year that you'd find me attending a service; despite being unable to locate a religious bone in my body, I'd always had huge respect for the sense of community that came from many faiths. I was also fascinated by the architecture of religious buildings, and this chapel was no exception.

The wider Charleton grounds formed part of the fabric of the space, through the pews that had been made from the wood of the trees off the estate. A glorious stained-glass window would, on a sunny day, throw a kaleidoscope of colours across the room. By the side of the magnificent alabaster altar stood a beautiful Christmas tree, an enormous star balanced on the top. A chapel volunteer was straightening some of the decorations and sweeping up fallen needles, the smell of fir floating through the air.

A large red bow had been attached to the end of each row of pews, and a wooden Nativity scene took pride of place in a far corner. I knew that the same stable and figures had been on display each Christmas for over 100 years. There was evidence of a couple of repairs, but it remained a lovely part of the chapel's history.

I always enjoyed visiting Father Craig Mortimer, the resident chaplain at Charleton House and a big bear of a man who practically filled any doorway he walked though. He had asked that I head over to the chapel for a chat. Despite not being a believer, I erred on the safe side and went with a little chocolate yule log and a piece of cinnamon shortbread. If I turned out to be wrong about the afterlife, then I wanted a man of God on my side.

'That better not be food, I've told you before you can't bring food or drink in the chapel.' The angry voice of volunteer Harriet Smedley shouted up the aisle seconds after I'd pushed open the heavy wooden door. Dammit, I'd meant to hide the bag.

'No, no,' I stammered like a naughty schoolgirl, which was exactly how I felt whenever I was in Harriet's presence. 'It's... paperclips. Lots of paperclips, Craig has run out.'

'I'll take those paperclips.' Craig's arm reached over my shoulder and took the bag. I hadn't heard him approach. He opened it up, smelt the contents and, with a smile, declared them, 'The best-looking paperclips I've ever seen, or smelt. Thank you.'

Harriet looked furious. She was a meddling, pedantic, irritating old woman, but she had eyes like a hawk and I was convinced there was more to her than any of us knew. She terrified me and fascinated me at the same time. Her choice of hats also entertained me, and today's was a brown and red close-fitting woolly effort that I assumed was meant to resemble a Christmas pudding. Maybe she had a sense of humour, too; I just needed to find further evidence of it. Yet another mystery for me to solve.

Craig led me out of the chapel through a small side door. For most of the last two years, his office had been a hobbit-like space in the concrete-lined basement amongst pipes and fuse boxes.

The refurbishment of the vestry was now complete and Craig had a smart set of rooms that included a meeting room and small kitchen, as well as his office.

'Come on through, I've just put the kettle on. A little birdie tells me you had an interesting night.'

'That little birdie gets around fast,' I observed.

'Is the little birdie right?' It was funny hearing such a big guy talk about 'birdies' with a voice better suited to conversations with a toddler.

'The little birdie is going to end up in a pie, but yes, the latest gossip is right. I've not heard anything more yet so I have no idea how old the skeleton is. It would be awful to discover that it's recent enough that we might have known them.'

Craig puffed as he lowered himself into his chair.

'I hadn't thought of that. I'm not aware of any of the congregation going missing, or even just local talk, but someone like Harriet would know. She has her uses.' He cut the chocolate log into pieces and slid the plate towards me.

'No, thank you, Father. I've already decimated our display of baked goods this morning.'

He smiled. 'Ably assisted by Mr Boxer, I'll bet. He needs fattening up – that skeleton probably has more meat on its bones than him. Look, I won't take up too much of your day, but I wanted to ask if you'd do a reading at the staff Christmas service. It would be lovely to have you involved.'

'Seriously? You know I'm not a churchgoer; it wouldn't be right.'

'That doesn't matter. For a lot of the staff, it's the only time of year they come into the chapel, bringing with them varying degrees of faith, and different kinds of faith, too. It's about bringing the Charleton House community together and sharing a special time of year in a special place. Everyone has a fondness for the house and a love for their neighbour – in this case, their colleagues. You're a well-liked, well-respected member of the

Charleton House community. In the time you've been here, you've already had a huge, and unusual, impact. I know that everyone would love to have you involved. Will you think about it?'

I nodded. 'Of course.' I was flattered, but it felt a bit strange.

'Great, so I'll add you to the list of speakers.' He grinned and took a huge bite of shortbread. 'God, this is good,' he muttered, spitting crumbs onto the desk.

It was strange being at the Black Swan when it was closed. The police had insisted that Steve keep the place closed for the day while they finished their work in the cellar, so Mark and I were sitting in his private kitchen at the far end of the building. Steve had opened a bottle of red wine and we were doing a great job of finding the bottom of it.

'I've only two couples staying and they're regulars who have been really understanding. I offered to make dinner for them and they could have room service, but they were happy to eat out. I'm going to give them a big discount when they go.'

I'd forgotten all about his B&B guests. 'Aren't they creeped out?' I asked.

'No, just curious. I'm pleased this didn't happen on a weekend when all the rooms were full.' He thought for a moment. 'It can't have been recent,' he mused. 'I've been here five years now and I've not heard of anything. I gave the last landlord a call this afternoon and he's drawn a blank, too. Could the skeleton have been put there to set someone up? To set me up?'

He looked at me like I'd know the answer. I shrugged.

'I don't know, but it would be a lot of work to pull off. Does anyone hate you that much?'

'I hope not. I always try and avoid confrontation; I need to keep my customers happy, so I tend to deal with problems before things get nasty. No, no one.'

Mark helped himself to a top-up of wine.

'I've not done any substantial research on the pub, but there are a few stories floating around about fights and violence over the centuries. I know there was a stabbing between two men who had a disagreement over politics – that was in the 1800s, I think, but neither of them died so it couldn't be one of them. This was also the pub where a young couple, hoping to get married, met their murderers.'

Steve looked surprised. 'I've never heard that one.'

Mark sat up straight in his seat and I knew he was getting into tour guide mode. 'There's a chapel not a million miles from here where young lovers could get married without the consent of their parents. It was within the boundary of a royal forest so the local priest could marry couples immediately without the need for banns – we're talking the 1700s, although the last wedding carried out in this way was in 1938.

'One young couple stopped here for something to eat and were overheard getting directions to the chapel from the land-lord. The three men who overheard them spotted the nice clothes they were wearing and guessed they were carrying a lot of money. Whilst the couple dined in another room, the men got rather drunk and were thrown out. They hung around until the couple left and then got ahead of them, waiting for them on the route the landlord had given them. They captured the couple and killed them. The murderers weren't caught, but a few years later one of them, a miner, was killed by falling rocks, one went insane and the third died after a fall from a horse, but not before he'd made a deathbed confession and named his accomplices.'

'Poor sods,' muttered Steve. 'I had no idea.'

'But no murders *in* the pub?' I asked.

'Not that I know of. Not off the top of my head, anyway, but it would be easy to find out if there were any stories in public circulation. Once we know how old the bones are, we might be able to narrow it down. There's tales like that all over Derbyshire

– plenty of pubs are meant to be haunted and have some great stories behind the strange goings on.'

'I thought you didn't believe in ghosts?' I said.

'I've never said that. I haven't seen one, but I believe that other people believe they have.'

'What about the ghost tours you lead?' asked Steve. 'Do you believe the stories you tell?'

'I've always said that our job is not to say whether the ghosts are real or not. Our job as guides is to tell the stories and allow others to decide for themselves. What we think doesn't matter; it's important to share the history of the house and the stories of those who lived and worked in it. If someone who worked there said they saw a ghost, then it's important we record their experiences. We're not here to judge.'

Steve nodded in approval. 'Nice bit of fence-sitting there. But come on, you've never heard anything? You've worked at the house for years.'

Mark shook his head. 'I have been with people when they've experienced something, but not me.'

'I hope I haven't disturbed more than bones. A ghost might be good for business, but it's not something I have any wish to run into in the dead of night when I'm changing over barrels.'

I couldn't have agreed with Steve more. I was fascinated by the idea of ghosts, but not over the road from my house. I looked at my empty glass and decided it was time to leave the chaps to it, before they started exchanging stories that would give me nightmares.

CHAPTER 5

*S*teve had called us the next morning, so almost twenty-four hours later we were back in the pub – but not because of an alcohol problem. DS Harnby had been able to use her contacts and get the report on the skeleton back quicker than usual, and she and Joe had arranged to talk to Steve about the findings. She'd wanted us there, too.

When Mark and I walked through the door, the two police officers were already sitting at a table and Steve was carrying mugs of drink over to them.

'Tea, coffee?' he offered.

'No thanks,' replied Mark, 'I'll wait until you can sell us the hard stuff.' It was four-thirty and the pub was reopening at five, so he didn't have long to wait.

Joe looked up and gave us a big beaming smile. I smiled back, but quickly looked away; I wasn't quite sure if I should have been behaving like nothing much had changed, or distancing myself a little. What was the look that Harnby just gave us? She and I had started to get to know each other better since the summer, but she appeared to be very much in 'serious cop' mode.

'Okay, let's get on,' she announced. 'Mark, I thought your local knowledge might come in useful. Sophie, I figured you'll start poking around at some point, so we may as well stop pretending and have you here as well. We'll say it's for local knowledge, too.' She didn't look happy, but I could have sworn I saw the corner of her lip twitch as she fought back a smile.

She opened a file and started summarising the report she pulled out. 'So, it's hard to give an accurate age. They can only get within about thirty to forty years, but we're looking at a male who died at least 100 years ago, and he was in his early fifties. We know he had a limp because he had a fractured femur that was never fixed; he also had gout, which would have added to that. Now, I'm not going into gory details, but it looks like his death wasn't accidental. It appears he was hit on the back of the head with something long and narrow, and was then pushed, or fell, into the cellar where he damaged the front of his head. It could have happened somewhere else, but in all likelihood it happened here.'

She looked up. If she wanted to check we were all paying attention, she needn't have worried. All three of us were staring at her, mouths slightly ajar as we took in the fascinating information. I glanced over at the fireplace where a long narrow poker was leaning against the wall.

'Well!' exclaimed Steve. 'At least it's not going to be someone we know. That's a relief. I mean, still awful, but at least it's not a regular.'

'Plus or minus thirty or forty years, so we're looking at what – 1870s to 1920s?' asked Mark. 'That's quite a big window.'

'How can you narrow it down?' I asked. 'There must have been all sorts of people who went missing around then, or people thought they'd moved away.'

Harnby smiled properly for the first time. 'That's where I'm hoping Mark can help.'

He looked up at her. 'I'm the first to admit I'm a pretty unique human being with remarkable talents, but I'm afraid I was off school the day they ran lessons on hundred-year-old skeletons.'

'It's not the body you can help with.' She opened the file again and pulled out a couple of photographs. 'You like a beer, you like history, you have a knack for soaking up utterly useless information like a sponge, so I'm told.' She glanced across at Joe, who had obviously been telling her about his brother-in-law in some detail. 'So, before I spend my time hunting down an archaeologist, can you tell me anything about these? They were found with the body.'

Mark took the photos from her and placed them in front of us. He pointed at a group of objects in the first photo.

'These are dead easy, no pun intended, and you don't need me for them. They're Victorian coins, pennies and sixpenny bits from the 1860s onwards. The most recent is from 1883; you can see the dates clearly, so we know he was killed after then. This…'

'That's a clay pipe,' I interrupted, quickly recognising the small, mottled grey object. The bowl where the tobacco went was still intact, but only about an inch of the stem remained.

'Very good, professor.'

'Now you've both identified the obvious things I didn't actually need help on, what about that?' Harnby pointed at what looked like pieces of a broken bowl or cup. They must have been given a good clean as the pretty baby-blue colour was clearly visible.

'Detective Sergeant Harnby, you really must try harder.'

'Go on, Mark,' she said with a slight groan. 'Tell us what's obvious to you, but not to us ill-informed police officers.'

'These are pieces of a china beer mug. Look at this stamp: VR 19. The VR is for Victoria Regina, so the mug was made during the reign of Queen Victoria. Nineteen is the number assigned to Derbyshire. Every county had its own number. After the Weights and Measures Act of 1878, any drinking vessel had to have a stamp to show that it was a recognised size. You know, pint, half pint, or quart. So this also confirms that he died after 1878.'

'I thought they all used pewter tankards in the olden days,' I said, remembering films where people were shown drinking out of shiny silver pots. Mark shook his head.

'I doubt it. They were actually fairly expensive so your average rural pub was unlikely to use them at that time. In some places, regulars had their own tankard behind the bar, but again I can't imagine that here. Low-paid agricultural workers, which is what we had a lot of in this area, couldn't have afforded that. They'd have struggled to pay for a drink some days, but if those pennies were the dead man's, then he wasn't a snecklifter. Or at least, not on the day he was killed.'

'Come again?' said Steve. I'd forgotten he was there.

'Snecklifter. Sneck means latch, so a snecklifter was someone who didn't have enough money for a drink and would lift the latch on the door to the pub and sneak a look to see if there was anyone they knew who could buy them one. It was sometimes used to describe people who could afford just one drink, but were then dependent on other people's generosity for another. They were sly, or crafty.'

'I've got a few of those now,' grunted Steve. It seemed some things never changed.

'Thanks, Mark, I'm impressed.' Harnby looked it, too.

The pub had opened while we'd been chatting and had started to fill. Steve looked over at the bar.

'If you don't mind, I should 'elp out.'

Harnby stood and shook his hand, and he left us to it.

'We should be going, too,' she said to Joe, who looked disappointed at the missed opportunity for a pint. She looked back at Mark and me. 'I realise there's little I can do to stop you carrying out research that might relate to this, but just don't do anything daft and don't get me in trouble. I will land on you like a ton of bricks if you make my life any harder than it needs to be.' She walked towards the door with Joe right behind. As she opened the door, she called back.

'And make me the first person you call if you find anything.'

Mark had just returned from the bar with a drink for each of us as Father Craig walked through the door.

'I'll be back with yours, padre,' Mark said before turning on his heel.

'I wondered if I'd find you both here, back the minute it opens.'

I laughed at his comment. 'Are we that predictable?'

'Come on, a skeleton in a pub? This is a dream case for you two. So, do you know who the victim is yet?' Craig raised his eyebrows and froze theatrically, waiting. I threw a beer mat at him.

'We've only just found out the first few details about the victim, and now we know he was a victim. It wasn't an accident.'

Craig shook his head sadly. 'Well, I hope you can find out who he was and what happened and he can be laid to rest properly.'

While we waited for Mark to return from the bar, I filled Craig in on our conversation with Joe and Harnby.

'Well, yours has been a more interesting day than mine,' he concluded. 'I've spent it playing referee and getting my ear chewed off. I love Christmas, but the run-up is a killer – sorry.'

'Who's been chewing your ear?' Mark asked as he placed a beer in front of Craig.

'A visitor was complaining about the Christmas tree in the chapel because it's a pagan symbol. I told him if we removed all pagan aspects from Christmas, there wouldn't be much left.' He took a mouthful of beer, leaving a line of foam attached to the top of his lip. Looking around the room, he waved at one of the Christmas trees. 'I love all this, the lights, the cheesy 80s Christmas music, but there's only so much enthusiasm I can muster for 'Away in a Manger' on the thirtieth time. I only started going to church cos I fancied the vicar's daughter. Look where that got me: single and eating more Christmas dinners over one Christmas than you two have had in a lifetime.'

The line of foam was still sitting on his top lip. I waved a paper napkin at him.

'Honestly, you need a woman in your life.' I pointed at my lip.

'What? Oh, cheers. Yeah, I guess that way I'd also get my laundry done and the only clean t-shirt I've got wouldn't be this.' He pulled up his sweater to reveal a t-shirt stretched across his rather large stomach with a picture of the Nativity on it. Underneath it said 'Spoiler alert, he dies'. Mark laughed so hard, I thought he was going to sprain something, and it was some time before I could stop laughing long enough to take another drink.

After we'd all calmed down, I remembered something Craig had said.

'Why have you had to play referee? Who's been fighting?'

'Some of the chapel volunteers. I left them facing off over the table, arguing about which mulled wine recipe to use at the volunteers' Christmas party next week.'

'Harriet Smedley?' I guessed. He nodded.

'One of the other party organisers wants to try something different. Smoking Bishop, it's called; it's port based. It was Charles Dickens's favourite mulled wine punch. It's a good idea really, especially as we have someone playing Charles Dickens and giving readings from A Christmas Carol for visitors. I think it sounds rather tasty, but Harriet wants to stick with the recipe she's been making for years.'

'How long?' Mark asked.

'I reckon Jesus had a taste,' Craig replied wryly. 'I'm a firm believer in tradition – I wear a frock for work – but I do believe in shaking things up a bit.'

'So you're going to tell her you're using a different recipe?' I was surprised at his bravery.

'Hell no, I'm not ready to meet my boss face to face just yet. They can decide amongst themselves. I'll let them fight it out and just hide the bodies later.'

CHAPTER 6

*W*ednesday morning was cold, and the grey clouds seemed to blend in with the steel-coloured sky. On days like this, the honey-yellow sandstone walls of Charleton House morphed into a grey shade of their own, in apparent sympathy with the elements. The building remained an impressive, imposing view; I just hoped that the heating was switched on inside.

I passed through the gate that gave staff access to a private lane behind the house and said good morning to the security officer on duty, turning as I heard the familiar sound of Father Craig's voice behind me. He was on his phone.

'I'm so sorry, Sian, just make sure you go to the doctor, or ask for a home visit if you don't think you can leave the house. You must let me know how you're doing. Promise me… Okay, bye.'

He hung up and looked at me with concern in his eyes. 'That's the fourth one this morning. They're all sick.'

'All who?' I asked.

'The four volunteers who stayed late last night planning the party. Apparently they all went home early feeling unwell, and all of them have spent the night being sick, amongst other things.

They think it's food poisoning, but it sounds pretty nasty. Sian doesn't appear to be quite as bad as the others; she was *so* apologetic because they didn't tidy up before they went. They just had to leave.'

I kept walking with him towards the chapel, wanting to help. Craig opened the door to the vestry, and just as he'd been told, the signs of the meeting were still on display. Files were scattered around the table; pens and notepaper remained in front of four chairs. Plates held cookie crumbs and four glasses held the remains of what looked like red wine.

I gathered up the crockery and glasses and took them into the kitchen while Craig put the files back on shelves. A large pan was on the stove. I lifted the lid: mulled wine. Was it Harriet's recipe or the new idea someone had been pushing for? I could still catch the whiff of cinnamon and cloves as I stirred the dregs in the bottom, wondering what might have upset the volunteers' stomachs.

'Santa came again.' Craig had walked in behind me, carrying a beautifully wrapped present shaped like a book. 'It's very nice having so many generous parishioners; it's a bit like being a teacher who gets lots of presents off the children at this time of year. But it can get a bit embarrassing, especially when they don't leave a label on it and I can't thank them. I've had a handful now, and I've no clue who left them for me. What have you found? Anything?'

I shook my head. Grabbing a small plate, I spooned out the fruit and spices from the bottom of the pan and put them next to the plate of leftover cookies.

'Cinnamon sticks, star anise, orange slices with cloves stuck in around the edges. That looks like fresh ginger, that's a cardamom pod, and I've no idea what those are.'

I fished out some red berries. They were a little like cranberries, but I'd never heard of those being added to mulled wine.

'Let me see those.' A female voice I didn't recognise came

from behind us and we turned round together. The slim woman was wearing a bottle green sweater that marked her out as part of the gardening team.

'Morning, Esther,' said Craig. 'This is Sophie Lockwood, Head of Catering. Esther Marsh is one of our volunteers; she also volunteers with the gardens team and does a lot of the flower arranging for us.'

Esther stepped between us and picked up one of the berries. After rolling it between her bony fingers and examining it closely, she looked around the kitchen until she spotted the small bin and lifted the lid, pulling out some little branches and leaves.

'Winterberries,' she said with confidence. 'Do you know who drank the wine?'

'Four of the volunteers,' replied Craig.

'How are they?' Her voice was calm, but I sensed concern.

'Not good, they're all sick.'

'Winterberries are poisonous. They're not going to kill you, but they'll make you very ill. They're also not something you'd find in a shop to use unaware of the risks. These must have been added on purpose.'

'I've never heard of them,' I said.

'Not many people have. They're fairly common, but very few people know what they're called, and even fewer know they're poisonous. You'll not generally see them in people's gardens, but on an estate like this, it's no surprise to find them. They're related to holly berries, which can also be poisonous. They sometimes find their way into Christmas decorations and you've got a problem if pets eat them, but generally people are clueless about winterberries. Unless you're a chapel volunteer.'

'What do you mean?' asked Craig. 'Why the volunteers in particular?'

'Remember the last talk I did for them a couple of months ago?'

Craig thought for a moment. 'You talked about your visit to

the poison garden at Alnwick Castle, and what we could find here at Charleton and in our own gardens. Esther, are you really suggesting someone added them to the mulled wine on purpose?'

'Not just the wine.' She walked past me and picked up the plate of leftover cookies. 'I bet that these aren't cranberry cookies. My guess is these are winterberries, too, and that was definitely not accidental.'

I pulled out my phone and scrolled to DC Joe Greene's number before handing it to Craig.

'The police are probably tired of hearing from me. You can make this call.'

I'd tried to keep out of sight once I knew the police were on the way. I was quite happy to ferret out information behind the scenes, and Harnby was increasingly coming to view me as a help rather than a hindrance, but I didn't want to push my luck. So, I was startled when I ran into Joe as I walked through the public routes and into the State Dining Room. He looked a little embarrassed to be found talking to Ellie Bryant, who was repairing the Christmas display on the large dining table.

'I'd finished talking to Father Craig and was just heading out. I happened to see Ellie,' Joe explained. The State Dining Room, which was definitely *not* on the way out and we all knew it, was a dark room with wooden panelling and tapestries sucking out any available light, but I would have sworn that Joe had gone red. Ellie just kept her head down.

'So, what do you think? Was it poisoning?' I asked. Joe looked around in case anyone was close enough to hear.

'At this stage, I don't know. We'd need to prove intent, that they knew the effect the berries would have. Which could be difficult.'

'Even with the workshop where Esther told a huge group of volunteers all of that?'

Joe shrugged. 'It could still be a challenge, and if anything, that makes it harder.'

I looked over at Ellie. She was working on a 3-foot-wide pie that took pride of place in the middle of the dining table at the centre of the room. It wasn't real, but a replica of an enormous Yorkshire Pie that the Sheriff of Yorkshire had sent to the 5th Duke of Ravensbury as a gift on Christmas Day in 1755. Part of the 'crust' had been removed to show the ingredients of pheasants, turkeys, plovers, snipes, woodcocks and partridges. In this case, models of the birds had been added, rather than featureless lumps of meat. It was rather fun, but one over-eager child had crawled under a barrier and attempted to pull out a plastic turkey. Ellie, who worked for the conservation team, had been asked to look at it at the same time as fixing the bird back in place in case anything of value on the table had been damaged.

It was only certain staff who were allowed 'behind the ropes', and they had different coloured staff passes to the rest of us to show that they were permitted to cross barriers and get close to the most valuable or delicate items in the house. I was pleased I wasn't among that number; I knew I'd break something within minutes.

I looked back at Joe; he was intently watching Ellie. He definitely blushed when he caught me looking at him. I laughed, but it was getting awkward so I decided it was time to leave.

'Well, okay, then. Keep up the good work, detective. Oh, and you might want to make sure that pie hasn't been poisoned.'

Both Joe and Ellie laughed. The atmosphere quickly relaxed, so I left before it could change again.

I was wiping down tables and moving chairs back into their rightful places in between looking at my watch and willing the last hour of the day on, when Mark came bounding into the Library Café.

'Well, that was easy!' he declared, looking extremely pleased with himself.

'What? Have you finally learnt the alphabet off by heart?'

'I'm in such a good mood, I'm going to ignore such an undeserved comment. Sit down and let me tell you a tale about a skeleton.'

I did as I was told while Mark undid the buttons on his waistcoat, made himself comfortable and pulled out a pile of notes.

'Ready?' He looked decidedly smug. 'It was easy enough finding out some general background on the Black Swan, or rather "the Plough" as it was known back then. Good job Bill reminded me of that or I'd have had a wasted morning.'

Bill, Mark's husband, was a retired rugby player who was now a history teacher and wasn't short of useful knowledge himself.

'Anyway, I had some really rough dates based on the fragments of the beer mug, and a few decades to work on because of the ageing of the skeleton. Also, the Plough wasn't the scene of a lot of fighting; it had its issues, but from what I can tell at this point in time, it was certainly better than some of the other pubs in the area, so there weren't stacks of reports of problems to plough through... plough through? Plough pub?'

Mark looked at me expectantly. 'I am wasted on you.' He sighed theatrically, and then carried on with his account.

'Well, in 1884 this changed and there was a fight. It got a lot of attention because it ended up in a brawl that involved pretty much everyone who was in the pub at the time. The landlord turfed them all out, the brawl continued outside and the police were called. That was that.

'Two days later, there was mention in the papers of a local man who had gone missing. He was last seen at the pub the day of the brawl. It was a really small article; it got just the one mention, and then nothing else. The man's name was Edwin Lee, or Dwin to his friends. Get this, the one identifying feature that gets a mention: he had a limp.'

'Really? That's fantastic! Have you told Joe?'

'No, not yet, I wanted to tell you first. I'll call him on my way home.'

'Was there anything else? Any family?'

'Not in this article, but there must have been someone who missed him after two days in order to report it to the police, although that could have been an employer. Maybe there was a wife who was pleased to get some peace and quiet, but then developed a guilty conscience.' He shrugged. 'I'll check out the parish records tomorrow, look at births, deaths and marriages, that sort of thing.'

I thought for a moment.

'If he was killed during the fight, then surely someone would have known. His body would have been left, and then found when the landlord was clearing up. If he fell through the trap-door, then his body would have been there for anyone who looked down to see. Surely he would also have been mentioned in the original newspaper report about the fight. He was tucked away in the corner of the cellar and we know his death wasn't accidental, so he wasn't just caught up in the melee and abandoned. What if he was killed around the time of the fight and the two things aren't related, or someone used the fight as a convenient shield for a targeted murder?'

Mark looked at me and nodded.

'I was thinking the same thing, Sherlock.'

CHAPTER 7

J'd lain awake for a while, trying to remember what routine tasks I had to do on a regular Thursday and who I could delegate them to. I was becoming adept at the art of delegation – a little unfair on my staff, but my attention kept being drawn by murder. I hadn't heard anything from Joe, but I was working on the basis that the mulled wine had been intentionally doctored and the four volunteers who were sick were a targeted audience, particularly as one of them was Harriet Smedley. A little surprised that someone hadn't tried to knock her off before, I was prepared to bet there were a lot of people who had wondered where they could quickly and easily hide a body in Charleton House after they'd had an encounter with her. There were plenty of options around the place; I wasn't immune to being wound up by a few of my colleagues, so I'd spent some time considering the options myself.

I was prepared to put money on Harriet being a morning person. I could imagine her bustling around her kitchen with whichever knitted hat she had opted for already firmly jammed on her head, and woe betide anyone who interrupted her rigidly performed routine. But I decided it was worth the risk, so after making a strong coffee in a travel mug and grabbing a slice of quiche I'd brought home the night before, I gave Pumpkin a cursory scratch behind the ears and dashed out of the door.

Harriet lived at the end of a row of workers' cottages. Her home was very similar to mine, only I had neighbours on each side of me. Despite all of the vibrancy being lost in a wet and grey English winter's day, it wasn't difficult to imagine the small front garden bursting with colour in the spring; it was very well tended.

The glass in the white front door glowed with the warmth of a lamp in the hallway. It felt welcoming, which immediately made me question whether I had the right house. I knocked tentatively, not convinced I actually wanted her to hear; that way I could leave and say I'd tried. But before I could try knocking harder, a small figure came scurrying towards the front door and flung it open.

'Yes?' she demanded, before staring at me intently. 'What on earth… why are you here? Sophie Lockwood, isn't it, from the cafés? Forever bringing food into the chapel.' So she remembered me, in detail. 'What are you doing here?' she asked again, looking unusually pale and tired, but her eyes were as bright and steely as ever. It would take more than berries to get Harriet down.

'I heard that you'd been unwell; I wanted to come and see how you were,' I lied. She stared at me.

'Rubbish! The police have been in touch, reckon it was poisoning. I know your reputation, you're wondering if I know who did it.' She held the door open and stepped back. I hesitated. 'Come on, then, I'm not doing this on the doorstep.' She bustled me towards the front room. My feet sank into a thick burgundy-red carpet; the cream sofa and armchairs were spotless. I wondered if they'd only just been delivered from a showroom; perhaps I would be expected to levitate above the pale fabric.

A small Christmas tree stood on a low table in front of the window, and above the fireplace hung a beautiful watercolour of Charleton House. I stepped closer, ignoring her offer of a cup of tea as my eyes explored the perfect detail of the painting.

'Who is the artist?' I asked as I peered at the initials. 'HS. Wait, is that you?'

'Well, Harriet begins with an H and Smedley with an S. That's normally how initials work. I won't have coffee in the house, nasty stuff, so it's tea or nothing.'

'Nothing for me, thank you.' I was still looking at the painting as I stepped backwards and sat on the sofa; I no longer knew who I was here to talk to. The irritating zealous guardian of all things chapel related, or someone with a delicate, romantic streak and a talent that should be shouted about, not tucked away above a fireplace. In the artist's home.

'You've not come here to see my paintings, so what do you want to know? Are there people out there who want to kill me, or at the very least make me spend a couple of days feeling sick as a dog?' I was about to respond, but she didn't need prompting. 'Of course, there are. Well, maybe not wanting me dead, but there's probably a queue of people experiencing a moment of glee about all this. I'm not stupid, I know what people think about me.'

'Doesn't it upset you?'

'Heavens, no.' She made it sound as if I'd asked a thoroughly ridiculous question. 'I've developed quite a thick skin over the years. That chapel is my second home; there isn't anything I wouldn't do for it, and it's given me solace and peace and strength in a crazy world for almost eighty years. I know every crack in the wood and chip in the plaster. That's what I fill my head with, not gossip. I've got God to talk to, and he talks a lot of sense.

'If I don't want you carrying your coffee through there, it's because I know what eighty years' worth of spilt drinks can do. I see the damage that mice do once they're tempted in by the crumbs from your damnable cakes. That's what matters, and I'll keep protecting the place – and the people, believe it or not – till the day they have to carry me out in a box.'

I stared at her as her words sank in. Her voice had the creak of an old woman, but it was strong and clear. With her close-cropped silver hair and neat blouse, the buttons fastened all the way up to the neck, she looked like an extremely determined and focused woman.

'I can't give you names of people who stand out more than anyone else, and if I did give you a list, it would be too long for you to do anything with. Anyway, I'm pretty sure the other three who were there have been rubbing people up the wrong way. Maybe you should look at them, Sian and Verity in particular, although that Kenneth Wexler probably encourages them. That might narrow it down for you.'

I knew nothing of the other three volunteers who had been at the meeting, except that one of them wanted to be in charge of the mulled wine. I couldn't believe I hadn't asked the obvious question.

'Harriet, who made the mulled wine?'

'I did, and one of my key ingredients is *not* winterberries.'

'What about the biscuits?'

'No idea. They were there when we arrived. We assumed that Craig had left them for us. As far as I know, he's never baked anything in his life, so we all thought he'd bought them, or another volunteer had made them.'

I was on the verge of asking about the other volunteers at the meeting when Harriet stood up. She seemed a little more weary than when I'd arrived.

'I think I need another cup of tea.'

'Of course, I'm sorry. You probably still need to rest.' I immediately felt bad; she was no doubt feeling a lot worse than she was
letting on. 'Thank you, Harriet. If there's anything I can do,
please, let me know.'

'Thank you, but that won't be necessary. I'm more than
capable of looking after myself.'

I didn't doubt that for one minute.

It was still early as I drove through the Charleton Estate. There
was a sliver of blue trying to break through between the clouds,
but I didn't hold out much hope for it. The sheep I passed all
looked resigned to another damp day and the house was yet to
recapture its glow.

As I got closer, I could see a little sprinkle of colour from the
rooms where a lit Christmas tree had been positioned near a
window. A tall, narrow tree had also been placed next to the
wooden box where visitors bought their car park tickets from a
member of staff, so well wrapped up I could only see their eyes. I
waved as I slowed down so they could see the staff parking pass
attached to my windscreen and made a mental note to send
someone out with some hot chocolate and a brownie to warm
him – I could only guess it was a him – up.

The Library Café was all set up and ready to go as I walked in,
grabbed two takeout coffees and a couple of pastries, and dashed
across a damp cobbled courtyard to Mark's office.

Mark was leaning in, staring at his computer screen as I
arrived.

'Get some glasses,' I told him, 'or you'll damage your eyesight.'

'I don't want to wear glasses and hide my natural beauty
behind some horrible plastic...' He trailed off as I dramatically
removed my own glasses and pretended to clean them.

'What were you saying about glasses?'

'Nothing.' He tore off a piece of pastry and shoved it in his mouth. Crumbs fell all over his desk. I opted not to wind him up any further and filled him in on my morning's visit with Harriet while he ate.

'Did you know she could paint?' I asked.

'I don't know anything about her, other than her remarkable ability to offend everyone who comes within fifty feet of her. It's hard to imagine her doing anything so delicate. Are you sure she wasn't just winding you up?'

'Sure.'

'Well, while you've been gadding about, I've done a bit of early morning research and apparently we have a diary in our archives that was written by a maid who worked here around the time Dwin died. One of the curators is checking on its location for me, and a couple of other things. I want to see if the Black Swan, or rather the Plough, gets a mention. So if you need me, I'll be tucked away in the corner of some dusty room.'

'You'll love it.'

He grinned at me. 'I know.'

'Sorry to disturb you, Mark, can I just get your bin?'

Mark jumped. 'Bloody hell, Peggy, I didn't see you come in.'

'Sorry, love, I didn't want to disturb you.' The cleaner reached under Mark's desk and tipped the contents of his bin into a large black bag, before moving on to the other desks.

'Peggy—' I'd had a thought '—don't you also volunteer in the chapel?'

'I do, my love. In fact, as soon as I've done here, I've promised I'll go and help put up some decorations in the vestry.'

Mark and I looked at one another. I wondered what she could tell me about the other three volunteers who had been taken ill, as I hadn't been able to follow up Harriet's comment with her before I'd left.

'What do you know about Kenneth Wexler?'

'What sort of thing?' She pulled out a chair and sat down.

'I heard that he and a couple of the female volunteers might have irritated some of the group. Do you know anything about it?'

Peggy laughed. 'You mean old Romeo? He's harmless enough, but those women, Sian and Verity, make such fools of themselves. They should know better at their age.'

Mark had perked up at the sound of some gossip and rolled his chair closer.

'Come on, Peggy, fill us in.'

'Well, I'm not one to gossip, but those two have been throwing themselves at Kenneth for months now. One of them's always baking something, but it just so happens that everything they bake is one of Kenneth's favourites. They're always hanging around him, complimenting him on his tie or his pocket handkerchief, trying to sit next to him when we have talks. If he offers to help on a project, you can be sure they'll be there, too.

'The other day, Sian was talking very loudly in front of Verity about how she'd run into him at the supermarket and they'd stayed for coffee in the café. She made it sound like a romantic date in a five-star restaurant. One day, he happened to say his favourite colour is purple – what were they both wearing for the next Sunday service? You've guessed it! He looked like he was sat between a couple of aubergines.

'It's all getting a bit much, to be honest. Some of us just try and avoid them, but others are getting very fed up of it all. I wish he'd just pick one of them and get it all over with.' She pushed herself out of the chair and picked up the black bag. 'Like kids, the lot of 'em.' She was about to leave when she turned back. 'And, Mark, I've fixed the broken handle on your Union Flag mug. I'll bring it with me tomorrow.'

'Thanks, Peggy, you're a darling.' He blew her a kiss, and then picked up his beeping phone to read the message that had come through.

'She's not your maid!' I retorted. 'You should fix your own mugs.'

'Yeah, yeah, listen to this, it's from Joe. They're treating the volunteers thing as attempted poisoning. We're going to be busy.'

CHAPTER 8

*D*espite wanting to spend the day finding out more about the volunteers, I had to do some actual work. The Duke and Duchess were planning to hold an exhibition of some of their finest paintings and sculptures in London the following summer, and the Duchess wanted me to be involved to ensure that the 'Charleton experience' would include the food we served at events and a pop-up café we were planning.

I was in a buoyant mood as I walked through the house, excited at the prospect of making a few trips down to London. I'd spent ten years working there before I'd moved back to Derbyshire for my current job at Charleton House. It had been quite a shift: hectic restaurants in a business district of London were a world away from one of England's finest historic houses.

I took the long route through the staterooms to admire more of the decorations. In the State Drawing Room, decorations had been influenced by the Delft tulipieres that could be found in a number of rooms around the house. To the untrained eye, tulipieres look like large, very odd blue and white vases with extra holes and narrow spouts around the sides, but these beautiful tulip holders aren't for cut flowers. Instead, the bulbs are placed inside them and the flowers grow up through the ornate holes and spouts.

The cobalt blue decorations of the tulipieres were extremely fine and pretty against the white background, and those were the colours that now decorated this room. Three tulipieres had been placed along the centre of the dining table, incredibly realistic artificial tulips within the holes. More of these tulips had been scattered all over the table. The Christmas tree in the corner, which was so large I'd never have got it through my own front door if I'd tried, had been hung with little blue and white china clogs, miniature Dutch town houses and a selection of blue and white baubles. The whole display was exquisite and made a feature of an object that a lot of visitors were curious about, but didn't take the time to investigate, distracted by some of the flashier ornaments or paintings instead.

'Excuse me, thank you.' A familiar face was trying to navigate her way past a large group of visitors. I recognised Esther Marsh, the garden volunteer, and she grimaced as she saw me.

'Crazy! I swear every Women's Institute group north of Watford is in here today. The car park is nothing but coaches. The average age must be around 102.'

We fell into step as we walked. I followed her as her dodges and weaves around visitors resembled a contemporary dance routine. As we reached a quieter corridor, I asked her if she knew anything about the four volunteers who had eaten the winterberries and who might have been targeted. She looked a little surprised.

'You must have heard of Harriet's reputation. It wouldn't surprise me if someone decided to vent their frustration on her. Whoever did it has clearly taken things too far, but it's pretty obvious she was the target.'

'What about the others? I've heard they might have done something to irritate some of the wider group.'

She was suddenly less keen to talk. We could hear the sound

of visitors behind us. I turned to see a large group of elderly men and women. They looked unnervingly like a stampede.

'I reckon they're on the way to your café. They've got a look in their eye that says "tea and a mince pie".'

I couldn't help but laugh; Esther was probably right. She marched off at great speed. It was time to get back to work.

Within twenty minutes, the café was full and my staff had pots of tea and plates piled high with mince pies on every table. As a rule, we don't do table service in the Library Café, but we'll make exceptions, and with this crowd it was just easier, and better for the elderly visitors who needed a sit down. A couple of them had opted for the date and orange scones, and after that dozens of them wanted them so we had another round of plates to deliver. It was fun, though, and we all bantered with the visitors and made sure they had a good time. One old fellow even went as far as to pinch my bottom, but the woman next to him smacked him so hard that I doubted he'd ever do it again, to anybody, for fear his life would get considerably shorter.

Eventually they were on their way, fed and watered. They swept out of the café in the same tsunami style in which they'd entered and left my team and me tired but happy.

'Is it safe to come in?' shouted a voice from outside. 'Have they all gone?' Mark poked his head round the door. 'I don't have a white flag, but will this do?' He waved a piece of blank paper in the air.

'Get in here, you plonker,' I replied. He did so and stood in the middle of the room.

'It looks like a bomb's hit it. Where should I sit? I want to make sure they haven't hidden a landmine under a table.'

I took him by the shoulder and steered him towards a small round table in the corner.

'Sit. I'll bring you a drink in a minute. I need to put my feet up, too.'

After I'd helped my team tidy up and served a couple more customers, I made Mark and me a mug of coffee each, grabbed a pile of papers from my desk and joined him.

'I can do some work out here,' I explained as I put everything on the table. 'What are you up to?'

'You'll love this. I've been perusing the diary of Mary Ollerenshaw. She was a maid here in the 1880s. Came here when she was fifteen. She kept a diary; a lot of it is very "I went here... I did this... today the cook shouted at me", but there's also some wonderful insights. It seems she had a bit of a crush on the Duke's son.'

'Which Duke are we up to at this point?'

'The 8th. Remember? He's the one that knew Charles Dickens.' We'd held a sleepover at the house the previous year and the character of Charles Dickens had made an appearance as the guest of the 8th Duke. 'His youngest son, George Henry Fitzwilliam-Scott, is meant to have been quite a looker, and a bit of playboy from what I've read. It's not surprising that some of the younger female staff fell for his charms. He could also behave like the proverbial "spoilt brat".' Mark turned the page in his notebook. 'Get this, one night he was struggling to open the window in his bedroom, and as it was so late none of the servants were around to help. What did he do? He picked up a log from the grate and smashed the glass.'

'That's one way of getting fresh air. Does she say anything about the Black Swan?'

'The Plough back then,' he corrected me. 'Yes, some of the staff would go there. Mary knew the daughter of the Plough's landlord, Catherine, and she gets a mention.'

'Anything about an old bloke with a limp who gets bashed on the back of the head, or is that asking too much?' I joked.

'Sadly not, but I have lots more to read so I'm hoping I'll find references to the people who used to hang out there.'

'I doubt they called it "hanging out" back then,' I said.

'Leaning against a bar drowning their sorrows, then. Do you want to hear more or are you going to pick me up on my choice of words?' He picked up his notebook and turned it to show me the scrawl-covered pages. 'I've been hard at work.'

'Clearly. Go on, then.'

'I did a bit of general research. Two months after the brawl that broke out at the pub when Dwin Lee was last seen, one of the men who is reported to have been there was arrested for murder and hanged. This rather unpleasant individual – Michael Hall, he was called – killed a man during another fight. He alleged the victim owed him money. So basically, there was a man at the brawl who didn't need much of a push to take someone's life.'

'Do you think he could have killed Dwin?'

'It's possible. I can't find any more reference to this man on the internet, but I'm going to keep an eye out.' He eyed the mail in front of me. I hadn't got round to going through my morning post. 'You're popular.'

'Not really. Most of it's Christmas cards from suppliers who want to keep in my good books.' I flicked through the pile in case anything looked important. The handwriting on what was clearly a Christmas card, postmarked London, brought me up with a start. It was handwriting I was familiar with, and that I'd hoped I'd never see again.

When I'd moved back to Derbyshire just over two years ago, I'd left behind a ten-year restaurant and café career in central London, a love-hate relationship with the city and a fiancé. A fiancé who had been arrested for stealing money from the restaurant we both worked at, and while he was at it, he'd been sleeping with one of the much younger servers. I hadn't seen or heard from him since the day he'd been arrested, and I hadn't wanted to.

I slipped the card to the bottom of the pile. Mark knew about my ex, I just didn't want to deal with it right now. Hunting down a killer and a poisoner was much more interesting, and a darned sight less stressful.

CHAPTER 9

$\mathcal{N}$ow that I knew the police were taking the poisoning seriously, my curiosity had moved up a gear. I couldn't disagree with Esther: I was sure that everyone was going to be pointing the finger at Harriet as the intended victim, but as much as she could irritate the hell out of people, poisoning her just didn't ring true, unless someone was seriously unhinged. It seemed to be taking things a bit far to poison multiple people in an attempt to get to someone who was basically just irritating.

I didn't know enough about the other volunteers who had been involved and I wanted to change that, despite the lecture I would undoubtedly get from DS Harnby. As soon as we closed the café at four o'clock, I jumped in my car. Kenneth Wexler seemed to be very popular with the volunteer ladies, and so I was hoping he wouldn't mind a surprise visit by another.

The building must have once belonged to a very wealthy family – think factory owner rather than aristocracy. It was a large double-fronted house with enormous bay windows on both floors that had been turned into flats. It was already dark and I could see coloured lights twinkling in one of the rooms; a beautiful Christmas wreath had been hung on the shared front door.

I rang the buzzer and was welcomed by a rather well-spoken male voice. Once I'd told him who I was, he buzzed open the heavy black door and I walked into a smart open hallway with a wide staircase straight ahead. The black-and-white floor tiles didn't show a scrap of dirt or dust and a polished black side table held a bowl of fir-scented potpourri.

A door opened in the far corner and a grey-haired man appeared.

'Sophie, I'm Kenneth. Come in.' We shook hands as I entered and he escorted me through to his high-ceilinged sitting room. Ornate covings, picture rails and a grand fireplace reflected the size and value of the building when it had been a single house.

Kenneth was tall and good-looking, but not breathtakingly so. He was a little more suburban than that. His salt-and-pepper beard was carefully trimmed; he looked as if he took real care of his appearance.

'Make yourself at home, I'll get us drinks. Coffee or tea?'

'Coffee, thank you.'

When he returned, he was carrying a French press. On his tray was a beautiful set of china cups and a matching jug containing cream. A bowl of sugar cubes completed the set. He looked at me and smiled, then didn't take his eyes off me. I started to feel a little uncomfortable.

'Is that one of Harriet's paintings?' I asked, as much to keep the conversation moving as out of genuine interest. A view over the Charleton Estate hung behind the sofa.

'It is. She might be a pain in the proverbial, but she can wield a paintbrush.'

'Does she know you have this?'

'Heavens, no! I wouldn't want to give her the satisfaction. I bought it anonymously at a charity auction.'

He stopped and stared at it for a moment, much as I'd done at the one on Harriet's wall. Her work seemed to have that effect.

'I think there's a lot more to that woman than meets the eye.' There was a touch of affection in his voice. 'But good luck to anyone who tries to get close enough to find out.' From the way he looked at the painting, I sensed a curiosity about Harriet herself, not just her work. He wasn't the only one. The more time I spent thinking about her, the more I wondered what else was hidden behind her badly knitted hats and her single-minded guardianship of the chapel.

'I doubt your visit is about art appreciation. How can I help?'

'Are you feeling better?' I asked.

'Ah, you're here about that. Yes, thank you. I'll spare you the details, but I didn't get very much sleep and was quite weak. My appetite started to return this afternoon, so I appear to be on the mend. You know the police came to speak to me? I couldn't tell them any more than they already knew.'

'Which was?' He looked a little taken aback. 'Sorry, that was a bit abrupt. I'm just really curious as to who might want to do this somewhere like Charleton. I always thought it was rather like one big family. A dysfunctional family, maybe, but…'

Kenneth laughed. 'Aren't they all? All families have their issues and Charleton is no different. You are, of course, assuming that this was an… inside job, isn't that what they call it?'

'And you think it might not be?'

'Now I didn't say that, and how could it have been achieved if it wasn't someone from within the chapel? I do wonder if Harriet crossed the line with someone, but this does seem a rather harsh response.'

'You don't sound too angry or upset,' I said. It was true, he was extraordinarily calm for a man who had just been poisoned. I wondered if this particular kind of calm could quickly veer into boring.

'Yes, I suppose I do. I used to drive my ex-wife to distraction.

She'd be tearing her hair out over something and I just wouldn't see the point, not if I didn't have any control. It's a waste of energy.'

'But you could influence the investigation, if you knew anything that would help the police.'

'And if I knew anything, I would have told them, Sophie. We were just four old biddies planning a Christmas party. Verity and Sian are both delightful women, extremely generous, very attentive; you'd have to be crazy to have a vendetta against them. And Harriet… well, that's a different matter. You'll be hard pressed to find anyone who hasn't joked about adding something to her tea. But I still find it difficult to fathom that someone would actually *do* it.' He put his empty coffee cup down and sat back in the armchair.

'Did you notice anything unusual, anything at all?'

He shook his head. 'As I told the police, there were a few of the regulars hanging around before the meeting – all of them good, solid volunteers – Father Craig and the four of us. The other volunteers left; Father Craig gathered his things, said goodnight and he was on his way.

'About half an hour in, Harriet poured us all a glass of mulled wine, brought the plate of cookies to the table and we carried on working. I thought Harriet had made the cookies to accompany the mulled wine. Not long after that, I was feeling rather uncomfortable – we all were, and had to bring the meeting to an abrupt end. Once I got home, I was well and truly feeling the effects.

'The evening was as bland as that, I'm afraid. No arguments, no grand entrances, no sleight of hand with the wine glasses, otherwise we wouldn't all have been unwell. Despite what anyone says, I don't think Harriet was involved, and it certainly wasn't any of the three of us.'

'The others that were with you, Sian and Verity, you know each other well?' I was hoping he'd admit to some sort of love triangle, but I knew it was a long shot.

'Reasonably. They're both lovely ladies and we've become quite a firm fixture.'

'Do they like each other?'

He looked a little confused. 'Well yes, of course. I mean, they certainly get on very well.'

'They're not...' I wasn't sure how to put this '...competition for one another?' Now Kenneth looked seriously confused. 'You're a very good-looking man. I wonder if perhaps they both have a deeper interest in your company.'

He threw his head back and laughed. 'Oh please, Sophie, that's absurd; I'm just a creaky grey-haired old man. I think my days of appealing to the ladies are long gone.' He smiled with amusement in his eyes, but his response felt rehearsed. My guess was this had been put to him before and his display of modesty was well-practised. The amused smile he now cast upon me could easily be used to woo the ladies; his easy confidence added to his appeal. I was sure he knew precisely the effect he had on others. But was it enough to make someone want to poison the competition? It was worth considering.

I drove back home trying to put together everything I had so far; it didn't take long. I had next to nothing, which was handy as I needed to concentrate on my driving.

The roads in this part of Derbyshire aren't exactly single lane, but in places they are a real squeeze for two cars to pass, and if you meet a lorry, you don't stand a chance. I often equate driving on these roads to playing a game of chicken. You keep going, wondering whether it will be you or the other driver who will give way at the last minute. It never feels dangerous; the bottom line is neither of you wants to cause an accident and you are usually going slowly enough that you could avoid one, but I imagine for drivers from other counties, it is all a bit unnerving. There are no street lamps either, so I had my lights on full beam, my finger hovering over the lever just in case I came across another vehicle and wanted to avoid blinding the driver.

But there wasn't a lot of traffic on the roads. The rolling hills around me were now shadows in different grades of grey, and the only way I was going to spot a sheep was if it bounced off my bumper, so I took my time.

With no evidence to mull over and a slow journey, I had more time than I wanted to think about the Christmas card that was unopened in my bag. I'd done a very good job of moving on from London life and the fiancé who can quickly be summarised with the words "cheating" and "thieving". The last time I'd seen him, he'd been in the back of a police car. I had no idea where he was now, whether at home or residing at Her Majesty's pleasure. I honestly didn't care, so long as he was hundreds of miles away from me. I had no idea what his card meant, and right now, I wasn't interested in finding out if there was any sort of explanation inside it.

As I drove past the Black Swan and parked the car outside my front door, I spotted Father Craig walk into the pub. I made a split-second decision: I was going to join him for dinner and see if Craig knew anything helpful about his merry band of volunteers.

Steve nodded a greeting at his newest regular, the old chap at the end of the bar, and then moved over to serve Craig, who ordered a stout so black it looked like tar. I stood next to Craig and ran my finger down the menu. It wasn't a hard decision to make and Steve beat me to it.

'Fish and chips?'

'Am I that predictable?'

'I could be polite and say no.'

I laughed. 'I'll take it as a compliment. I'll have a glass of the usual as well.'

I was working my way through the pub's list of over seventy gins and we'd got into a routine of Steve choosing one that I had yet to try. It added an element of surprise, which seemed even more important if I was getting a reputation for being predictable.

'Father, are you meeting someone or can I pick your brains?'

'If you can find them, they're yours,' he replied.

We settled in at a small table next to one of the Christmas trees.

'Cheers,' Craig offered. 'Here's to presuming our drinks haven't been poisoned.'

'I doubt it, Steve would lose a large portion of his profits if he knocked one of us off. I went to see Harriet and Kenneth today.'

Craig smiled. 'I know. Well, about Harriet; she told me.'

'She came into Charleton? Was she okay?'

'Towards the end of the day, yes. She's fine. It'll take more than a handful of berries to bring that old girl down. I reckon she spends more time in the chapel than anywhere else anyway. It's her equivalent of staying at home. Did you find out anything useful?'

I shook my head. 'No, not a thing. Although Harriet did say something about Kenneth and the two women annoying some of the other volunteers. Peggy talked about it, too. Do you know anything about that?'

We paused for a moment while my fish and chips were placed in front of me. I added a good squeeze of ketchup and mayonnaise and plenty of salt, but no vinegar. If someone wants to prevent me stealing chips from their plate, adding vinegar is the way to do it. I can't stand the stuff.

Craig waited until I was done before answering. 'Kenneth joined us about eighteen months ago. It was a little awkward at first. He was an accountant and his old business partner has been part of the congregation for years. I believe they parted on bad terms. But Kenneth is an extremely nice chap, quickly became very involved and has helped me out a lot. His business experience has come in handy, and he's been on the board of a number of charities, so he's been really useful, going over some accounts with me, helping me understand aspects of tax law, that kind of thing. I'm useless at that and I was getting a bit embarrassed by how often I had to call the finance department for help. Kenneth's here three or four times a week.

'He also gives excellent readings; there's something about his voice that is perfect for the acoustics of the chapel. Doesn't hurt that he's quite good-looking, gave some of the ladies a bit of a burst of enthusiasm. Went out with a couple of them.'

'Verity and Sian?'

'No, they started hovering around him later.'

'So it's true they have a bit of a thing for him?'

Craig laughed, and then drained his pint glass. 'I'm usually oblivious to that kind of thing, but even I've noticed, yes, he does rather have his own fan club. Where he goes, they go, one on either side like a pair of bookends.'

'Are they good-humoured about it all or are they genuine competitors for his attention?'

'They both look friendly enough; they've become an inseparable trio, but I'm not convinced. There's something about their dogged loyalty to him that makes me think that behind it all, they're both scheming, in it for the long term with a very clear game plan. I'm sure he has quite a bit of money tucked away, and call me cynical, but that could set a woman up for her remaining years and pay for a lot of cruises.'

He thanked Steve, who had spotted his empty glass and come over to swap it for a full one.

'Could that game plan involve poisoning the competition?'

Craig didn't flinch. 'But they were all sick. It doesn't make sense to poison yourself.'

'Unless you either fake it, or you're prepared to put up with a day or two of illness for the sake of ensuring you're not viewed as a suspect. It would be the perfect cover.'

'But they also poisoned Kenneth. If they were in love with him, why would they do that?'

I thought about it for a minute; it was a good point.

'Another sacrifice that was viewed as proportionate? A chance to show him who is the best at nursing him? Perhaps the poisoner was frustrated with him for not having chosen them as his favourite and wanted to make him suffer. Two birds with one stone.'

'But they poisoned Harriet as well,' Craig reminded me.

'Hmm, make that three birds with one stone.'

CHAPTER 10

'*H*e beat us by about twenty minutes.'

I'd opened the window from the Library Café kitchen out onto the back lane when I'd seen DS Harnby walk by. It was very early on Friday morning and it was a little while until any visitors would arrive.

'We got the call from Mark to say the skeleton was Dwin Lee, and shortly after that, Joe walked into my office proud as punch, having identified the victim. I rather took the wind out of his sails when I said the name in perfect sync with him.'

'Poor Joe.'

'Nah, keeps him on his toes. I don't want him getting too cocky.'

'I can't picture him as cocky,' I said, a bit surprised that anyone would see him that way.

'True. Well, still, it keeps him in check.'

I couldn't tempt Harnby in for a cup of coffee. She'd made a visit to the house to catch up with Father Craig before the weekend, but now had another appointment to go to.

'Have you managed to find out anything else?' I asked.

'I'll be honest, Sophie, a 130-odd-year-old murder isn't the best use of our resources right now. We're stretched thinly enough as it is. We've done a quick check and we can't find any surviving relatives; the press attention at the start of the week didn't bring anyone out of the woodwork, so it's on the back-burner. As and when things crop up, we'll take a look.'

'Soooo...' I said, trying to ease my way into my next question, 'if we were to sniff around a bit and find out something of interest, we couldn't be accused of getting under your feet?' I did my best sweet smile and hoped I could charm her.

She laughed. 'I've been working on the basis that you're already well ahead of us. So long as you don't do anything illegal, stay out of trouble and my boss doesn't get wind of it – oh, and just remember that Joe is paid to work for the police, not you, so don't go taking up his time during work hours.'

She'd made my day. I wouldn't have to waste time making up excuses or trying to convince her I was 'just curious'.

She went to leave, but turned back again. 'I believe it might be worth making an appearance at the staff Christmas service.'

'Why's that?' I asked.

'There's going to be a star turn that I fancy seeing.'

'Who are you... hang on, what's Craig said? Has he told you I'm doing a reading?' She nodded. 'I'll kill him! I haven't agreed to it yet. I hate standing up in public; I get all tongue tied and start sweating – it's not a pretty sight.'

'You'll be fine. It's a friendly crowd, they'll want you to do well.'

'I wouldn't be so sure. There seems to be a poisoner in the midst of the chapel community. They're not all as well-meaning as they look.'

'You'd think attempting to knock off a couple of pensioners would be a waste of time; you just need patience and they'll pop their clogs soon enough.'

I laughed. 'I guess that's not the official police line.' I was gradually getting to see the other side of Harnby. Who knows? Maybe one day I'll be calling her Colette!

'Is she through here?'

Joyce wasn't asking a question of my staff; she'd never give them time to answer. Instead, she burst into the kitchen.

'I thought we were a partnership!' she demanded.

'A… a… what?' I stammered.

'A partnership. It wasn't so long ago you were begging for my help with a murder. Now you have two cases and I haven't heard a peep out of you.'

I didn't quite remember things the same way, and I certainly had no recollection of any begging. The last time I'd got caught up in a murder case, I had indeed had Joyce's assistance, but that was because Mark had ridden a bike into a tree and finished off up to his elbows in plaster. I was getting a bit concerned by Joyce's enthusiasm, and her increasing penchant for threatening violence with the heel of her stiletto shoes. Mark and Joyce had very different skillsets, if you consider charming blokes into giving evidence with an eye-popping cleavage a skill. It was certainly something that Joyce put to good use.

She leaned against the doorframe with one hand on a hip.

'What on earth are you doing? I hope some of them are for me. Wait, on second thoughts…' She bent over the table and took a closer look at the various gifts I was wrapping in polar-bear covered paper. 'What's this?' She held a pack of three furry pink balls. 'And this? Catnip?'

'They're for Pumpkin's stocking.'

She gave me a stern look. 'Hmm, on work time, no less. You are hardly leading by example, Miss Lockwood.'

I knew she was joking. 'When else am I meant to do it? I can't do it at home – she always wanders in when I'm wrapping presents. She likes to play with the paper.'

Joyce looked decidedly confused. 'And that's a problem because?'

'Because they won't be a surprise! She can't see her presents before Christmas Day.' I couldn't understand why Joyce needed an explanation; it was entirely logical to me.

Her eyes locked on to mine; she didn't blink. 'Are you entirely deranged? She's a cat. A cat. She's cute, I'll give you that, but I'll say it again. A cat.' She shook her head. 'Well, I just hope you got her the best catnip money can buy. If you insist on going to all this trouble, you better make it worth your, and her, while. I need a drink.'

I looked at my watch. It was at least thirty minutes since my last coffee: time to top up my caffeine level and ensure it wasn't being diluted by anything less essential, like blood or water.

'Coffee?'

'Sadly, that will have to do,' she said. The kitchen door swung closed, narrowly missing my face, as Joyce marched ahead, shouting over her shoulder, 'Don't even think of bringing a plate of bloody mince pies. I'm sick of the sight of the damned things.'

I mouthed *'Sorry'* to some customers. Tina, the Library Café supervisor, told me she'd get it and to go and sit down.

'No...'

'Mince pies,' Tina interrupted Joyce's shout. 'I heard. The whole of the estate heard.' She rolled her eyes and swung into action.

Joyce had taken a seat in front of the fire. Even I had to remind myself that it wasn't real from time to time. I'd placed a row of wooden reindeer along the top of the mantelpiece – simple and stylish, I'd thought, but Mark had already asked if they were kindling ready to be added to the faux flames.

'So what do you need from me?' Joyce asked before I'd sat down. 'This is one of the busiest times of the year in the shops, but the bonus of being in charge is delegation, lots of it. That'll free me up to help you.'

I let her ramble on about how I couldn't rely on Mark for anything useful. One day, she's going to openly declare just how fond of him she is, but I'm sure I have time to buy the thermals I'll need for when hell freezes over.

'Joyce, you look delightful.' Tina had arrived with our drinks and two slices of stollen. The rich German fruitcake is another of my festive favourites, although I never fail to cover myself in icing sugar when I eat it. 'It brightens up our day when you drop by,' she continued, with no obvious irony in her voice. 'If there's anything else I can get for you, please call. No, just click your fingers, save your vocal cords.'

Joyce just stared at her. I bit my lip; I wasn't sure if I was going to have to read Tina the riot act or congratulate her on her performance. She was brilliant at her job, utterly unflappable and a calming influence over my younger staff. I wondered what had got into her.

'Kill 'em with kindness,' she whispered to me as she walked off.

As Joyce enjoyed her stollen and turned her chest into a snowy mountain scene with the icing sugar, I filled her in. I seriously doubted there was anything she could add when it came to Dwin Lee; her historical knowledge was limited to the development of the high-heeled shoe, so I was surprised when she asked me if I knew the Black Swan had once been called the Plough.

'Yes, but how do you know?'

'I knew the last landlord quite well. We went on a couple of dates, but it didn't come to anything. Nice man, but I got tired of spending our dates sat at the end of the bar, waiting to snatch a few minutes with him between customers. He knew quite a bit about the history of the pub. He never said anything about a murder, though.'

'He didn't know about it, Steve already asked him, but we didn't know who the body was at that point. Anyway, Dwin vanished into thin air, end of story, or at least that's what people thought.'

'I still have Eric's number somewhere.' Joyce started to scroll down the names in her phone. I was fascinated. Her nails are long enough to double up as letter openers, and yet she's able to use a smartphone, and her emails contain fewer typos than mine.

She tapped 'call'.

'Hang on,' I said. She dismissed me with a wave of her hand.

'Hello there, Eric, so my number is still in your phone,' she purred. 'I'm well, thank you... I was wondering if you might like to catch up. I'm carrying out an investigation and you might be able to help... yes, I'm branching out... I'll bring my assistant, she can take notes.' I stared at her with bug eyes and she dismissed me with another wave. 'Wonderful, I'll see you at 4pm, on the dot.'

'Since when have I been your assistant?' I demanded with incredulity. 'Take you anywhere and there's an increasing risk of violence. I wouldn't stick you in charge.'

'Calm down, dear. Apart from the fact that you couldn't do your sleuthing without me, it's me he wants to see, not you. I need to make him think that he's confiding in the woman he finds irresistible. If you're just a lackey who keeps herself in the background, then he'll be more inclined to open up.'

'Open up about what? We want some historical knowledge, not his bank details.'

'Still, it's important I play a lead role.' She clicked her fingers in the air. 'I fancy another of those fruity things.'

I feared Tina – and I – had unleashed a monster.

CHAPTER 11

*E*ric poured us both a glass of prosecco. He had a good memory: it was Joyce's favourite and she willingly accepted her glass. I politely sipped at mine, knowing I'd be heading to the pub later, when I'd start my Friday night properly.

'So, what's this about an investigation, eh?' He glanced at me, but turned his attention swiftly back to Joyce, looking bemused. He was a round man – everything was round: his head, his belly, his hands all had a slightly inflated quality to them. Even the Jack Russell that snoozed by the side of his armchair looked as round as it was long. But Eric wasn't unattractive; he had a wonderful, warm smile. It seemed too obvious to call him jolly, especially at this time of year, but that's exactly what he was. When I'd first seen him, I couldn't quite understand Joyce's attraction to him, but gradually I was realising how it would be easy to fall for someone so warm and cheerful.

'It was a lovely surprise to get your call, Joyce. Every time I open a bottle of fizz, I think of you. Are you still working at Charleton House, or are you some sort of private investigator now?'

'Still at Charleton,' she declared. 'They'll have to carry me out of that place. I'm – we're – doing a little work on the side. Satis-fying a curiosity, you could say.'

'Well, I'll gladly help if I can. It wouldn't have anything to do with the skeleton they found in the Black Swan cellar, would it?'

'It would,' I answered. 'Joyce said you knew quite a bit about the history of the pub, is that right?'

Joyce scowled at me from behind her glass.

'The plan was to write a history of the Black Swan, but I never got round to much more than some fairly basic research. The skeleton's from the 19th century, right? I think that's what I read in the paper.'

'Yes, late 1880s,' I said.

'Okay, so that would make William Austin the landlord at the time. Not the most successful businessman, but he was able to keep afloat for about ten years. It changed hands when he died.'

'Unusual circumstances?' I asked.

'No, I don't think so. There was never anything said about it. His wife had died long before he took over the pub, and his daughter, Catherine, died in childbirth, poor thing. Not uncom-mon, of course.'

'What about the child?' Joyce finally chipped in.

'Died at birth. They're buried up at St Anne's church.'

I felt a thrill of excitement. If the gravestones were still in place, then I would be able to find a tangible connection to the Austin family, and therefore to Dwin. I was going to find them, whether or not it answered any questions.

Eric flicked through an old notebook. 'I don't have masses on that time. Austin was forever in debt, I know that much. He still was when he died.'

Joyce had sat back and was focusing on her wine while Eric and I chatted. It hadn't taken him long to work out that Joyce hadn't been quite accurate in her description of her role in all of this.

'Did Dwin get a mention? Dwin Lee?'

He thought for a moment, and then smiled. 'I know that name, and I know why.' He got up and searched through a bookcase that was so full, books were lying on the top of books and there was a pile next to it on the floor. He pulled out a small white book, *Myths and Mysteries of Derbyshire*, and searched for a page before handing it to me.

'*Edwin Lee was a quiet, well-respected local man who had grown up in the area. A framework knitter by trade, he was a religious man and attended St Anne's chapel regularly. He was a favourite with local children who called him "Uncle Dwin"...*'

'Does that help?'

I skimmed through the rest of the short chapter that went on to describe the unsolved mystery of his disappearance.

'Brilliant. It tells me what kind of man he was.'

'Take it.' He handed me the book.

'Are you sure?'

'Yes, you can still get it in local bookshops. That's all I have, I'm afraid. I hope it was worth the visit.'

I gave Joyce a gentle kick.

'What? Yes, yes.'

Eric gave me a knowing smile. My phone beeped.

'Sorry, I should have turned that off.'

'It's fine, it might be important.'

It was Mark. '*Meet at pub, ASAP.*'

'Not really, but we should go. Thank you, Eric, you've been really helpful.'

I looked over at Joyce. She refocused just in time.

'Yes, very helpful.' She handed him her empty glass. I kept an eye on her as we left – her handbag was big enough to hold the opened bottle of wine and I could do without her finishing it off on the drive home.

. . .

Mark was holding court at the bar when we arrived at the Black Swan. A group of middle-aged women with matching Christmas sweaters were being regaled with tales of the 5th Duchess of Ravensbury's gambling habit. When he saw us, he raised his glass in our direction.

Our usual table was already taken, so I grabbed hold of Joyce to prevent her from going over and bullying the customers out of their seats. When Mark had finished his performance, the three of us squeezed around a tiny table next to the bar.

'While you two skived off work early, I stayed late and did some more research,' Mark told us. 'Turns out the landlord at the time, William Austin, owed money.'

'We know,' Joyce and I chimed together. Mark looked disappointed.

'Oh, how do you...'

'Because our skiving wasn't skiving,' I replied. 'Well, it was, technically. We should have been at work, but we were doing our own research.' I raised an eyebrow at Mark and attempted to look superior. I'm sure I just looked ridiculous.

'He also had a daughter,' continued Joyce, 'who died in childbirth, along with the child.'

'Poor nipper.' Steve had arrived with a tray of glasses. The hot deep-red liquid had steam rising from it. 'Thought you might fancy some mulled wine, liquid Christmas spirit.'

I glanced up at Steve, asking, 'You haven't used winterberries, have you?'

'Never 'eard of em. Should I get some in?'

'God, no!' I cried.

'Oh, okay.' Looking confused, he pulled up a chair and sat just outside our circle, straddling it like a cowboy. 'Carry on, I'd love to know what you found out.'

'Do you have any more gems?' Mark asked Joyce. 'Or is it my turn?'

Joyce mimed handing him a microphone.

'After reading the diaries, I wanted to find out a bit more about some of the servants. I think it would make a fantastic tour in the future – visitors love all that behind-the-scenes stuff. I wanted to know what some of them were paid – it'll be the first question I'll get asked – so I started going through the ledgers. George kept cropping up; he seems to have been on the profligate side.'

Joyce screwed up her face.

'A big spender,' I whispered.

'Who's this George?' asked Steve.

'George Henry Fitzwilliam-Scott, the youngest son of the 8th Duke,' Mark told him. 'For some reason, he paid money to William Austin, who owned the pub back then.'

'Why? Would he have helped him out with debts?' I asked. Mark blew on his mulled wine before tentatively taking a sip, then continuing.

'It wasn't entirely uncommon for the Fitzwilliam-Scott family to invest in local businesses. They wanted to appear charitable and usually they got their name on a building, or an organisation was named after them in return. Also, if their local businesses were doing well, it was good for their own reputation. You don't want some scruffy rundown village on your estate, or nearby.

'George could have just been showing off. I get the impression he was a bit flashy. I couldn't see him linked with many official charitable organisations, so I wonder if it only tended to happen after he'd had a couple of drinks in him and started throwing his cash around. I'd love to know more about him. He sounds like a real character.'

'We found out something else as well,' I said. Mark looked intrigued. I pulled out the little book that Eric had given me. 'We've got some background on Dwin Lee.' I read him the short chapter that related to the man we were all so interested in.

'Let me have a look.'

I passed Mark the book.

'How have you not seen it? I thought you were interested in local history. Call yourself a historian,' Joyce said with scorn in her voice.

'Strictly speaking, I don't,' Mark replied defensively. He waved the little book at us. 'There are hundreds of this sort of thing; they're made for the tourists who just want the basics and to feel like they've learnt something without doing any real work. You know the kind: they visit Charleton House and spend more time in the gift shop and café than the house or gardens. I wouldn't waste my time with these things.'

He waved the book in the air again before putting it down on the table.

'Snob,' I offered. 'Is there any reason why the information in there would be incorrect?'

He flicked to the back to look at the author biography.

'I guess not, it's probably fine.'

I looked up just in time to see Joe Greene walk into the pub, Ellie Bryant with him. He waved at us.

'Ah, love's young dream,' Mark said, but not loud enough for them to hear. Joyce looked over at me.

'Are you going to be alright?'

'Me? Why? We were never actually dating. It's fine, *really*.'

'I think it's time I left you lot to it.' Steve swung his leg back over the chair and returned it to a nearby table.

'So, the field is open and we need to find Sophie a Christmas date,' declared Joyce.

'You'll do no such thing. I'm perfectly happy as I am. What about you? Your diary seems to have been unusually quiet on the date front.'

'I'm waiting to see who Santa leaves under my tree.'

'What about the fella over there? He'd be within your age bracket.' We followed Mark's eye line; he was talking about the old chap who had taken to sitting at the end of the bar most nights.

Joyce's head turned back slowly and, regarding Mark through narrow slits of eyes, she told him, 'That's *your* future date, Mark Boxer, once Bill realises he can do a whole lot better and ditches you for a higher quality model.'

'Children, time to stop fighting,' I scolded them. 'Mark, get the next round in.'

'Why me?'

'For being rude to your elders.'

Joyce looked confused as she slowly realised I wasn't being entirely complimentary about her. Once Mark had left the table, she swivelled her chair round to face me.

'Are you sure you're okay about Joe? Only I thought he would have been perfect for you. You would have made an adorable couple.'

'I'm not sure that "adorable" is the best motivating factor when choosing a life partner. Yes, I'm fine. Ellie is a lovely girl.'

Joyce nodded, looking decidedly unconvinced. I thought about the unopened Christmas card in my bag. I wasn't entirely sure I was going to open it at all. But I didn't want to leave it on my desk for prying eyes.

'Drinks, ladies, and Joyce, we have a solution for the endless quest that is your love life.' Mark was back and clearly feeling brave.

'What's that?' she asked sternly.

'Steve has got a knee-high plastic pear tree on the bar. It's full of little turtle doves and milking maids, that sort of thing. I reckon he'd loan it to us.'

We waited for him to continue.

'You've not heard of the Christmas tradition? If a girl walks backwards three times round a pear tree on Christmas Eve, she'll see the spirit or image of the man who will become her husband. I think it's worth a try.'

'Sophie, dear, next time, it's a girls only night, and the time after that, and the time after that.'

I laughed and Mark pretended to look hurt.

'I'm only trying to help.'

'I know, dear. In your own twisted, ridiculous way, I know you are.' She patted his arm. I changed the subject.

'When you two have finished kissing and making up, Mark, I've always fancied seeing the… what did you call them once? The muniment rooms. Would you take me?' I had a picture in my head of weird and wonderful artefacts on shelves in a series of creepy corridors.

'Sure, but we never call them muniment rooms now; they're just the stores or archives. I was thinking of going and having a look tomorrow.'

'It's Saturday.'

'I know, want to meet me?'

'Sure,' I said, a little more enthusiastically than I'd intended. There was so much of Charleton House I had yet to see and these rooms were near the top of the list. And like Joyce's, my appointment diary was full of nothing more than cobwebs.

CHAPTER 12

I was up bright and early. Well, I was bright; the weather was contradicting my mood, and low mist blocked my usual bedroom window view across the fields.

Pumpkin had clearly taken a look out the window and decided that sullen and miserable was the way to go. She lay at the end of the bed, apparently willing me to get up and leave her to it. Any attempt at affection on my part was greeted by a cross between a squeak and a snarl. Even a polite meow was beyond her. She didn't follow me downstairs for food, but like the good servant I am, I prepared her breakfast and refreshed her water anyway. I shouted goodbye as I left, which I know sounds ridiculous, but if she was already in a bad mood, I didn't want to risk making things worse.

Charleton House seemed to be at sail on a sea of mist as I drove slowly along the estate road, wary of what might leap out at me with little or no warning. I bypassed the cafés – my staff didn't need to know I was in, I'd only get dragged into a customer complaint or requests for leave, regardless of whether or not it was my day off – and walked down a stone corridor that was open to the elements, and smelt of cinnamon and fir.

This part of the house is one of the few places where you can see evidence of the original Tudor building, and set within the 16th century red bricks are casement windows with lattice lead work, the glass rippled. Signs of Christmas were evident here, too, and on each of the stone windowsills sat a small fir tree, decorated with slices of dried oranges, cinnamon sticks and delicate gold ribbon. They were all standing on a piece of hessian sacking that set them off nicely and gave the display a slight Tudor feel. I knew there were essential oils tucked away within the decoration to enhance the scent, something that wasn't allowed inside because of the risk to surfaces or displays from the oil, but out here we could breathe it in and it was one of my favourite of all the decorations around the house.

Father Craig was coming out of the chapel, and as I reached him, he was pushing the large wooden door closed behind him.

'Good morning, Sophie, you're looking rather... country.' I'd decided that if I was going to spend the morning going through the muniment rooms of a stately home, I wanted to look the part and had opted to wear a tweed blazer that rarely made it out of my wardrobe. I already had the bookish glasses; in fact, without them I couldn't see the book, let alone the words on the page.

'Morning, Father. Another gift?' He was holding a rather beautiful leather notebook that was still half wrapped in Christmas paper.

'Yes, it was on my desk this morning, with no note, as usual. It's starting to get rather silly; I'm feeling a bit uncomfortable about it all.'

'Do you lock your office when you leave?'

He shook his head. 'No, my clerk uses it, too, and I'm happy for the volunteers to use it when I'm not around. Anything important is locked away, it's all perfectly safe.'

'Maybe you should start locking it.'

'They'd only leave the gifts elsewhere, and I want it to feel like a friendly, open place. A feeling of trust is important within our community. Plus I'm not actually at risk. It's just odd.'

'How are the four volunteers? Are they all better?'

'They're fine. They were all in yesterday. Of course, no one will touch any biscuits that are brought in now.'

'Morning, Father, hello, professor.' Mark had joined us and looked me up and down. 'Nice jacket, you should wear that more often. I reckon we could buy you a PhD off the internet. Ready? I have the key.'

I was about to follow him when I remembered something.

'Sorry, Father, I forgot to say: drinks at mine tonight, if you'd like to join us. Seven o'clock?'

He looked very pleased with the offer. 'I'm up for that. And you've not forgotten my cookies, have you? The gingerbread?' I'd promised to make him 120 Christmas-themed gingerbread cookies that he wanted to give away in little gift bags at an event he was hosting.

'Of course not, Father, they're at the top of my to-do list.'

'Great, you're a star. Thanks.'

'You'd forgotten, hadn't you,' Mark whispered to me as we walked off. I looked at him out of the corner of my eye.

'Ye of little faith, Mark Boxer... Of course I had.'

Mark led me past the chapel, along more cloisters, round a corner and behind a rather frayed rope that had been hung at the bottom of a stone staircase to keep visitors out. I held on to the worn banister as I pulled myself up three flights of stairs; I could have sworn I was running out of oxygen as I reached the top. My policy of 'it's Christmas, I'll eat anything I want' wasn't helping my fitness levels, limited as they were at the best of times.

The staircase itself got more tired looking the further we went, and the pigeon poop more plentiful. I could spot four nests in the various alcoves and ledges. Mark opened a big, clunky door with a large key and held it open for me. I was surprised to find myself in a light, airy room. It wasn't in great condition – paint was peeling off the walls in places and the lamps needed dusting for cobwebs, but someone was clearly doing their best to make the room a pleasant place to work. But I was disappointed to find the grey metal shelves were full of large leather books and box files. There wasn't a single sword or stuffed animal to be found.

'You need to go to the Hunterian Museum in London, you freak,' retorted Mark when I commented on the lack of body parts in jars.

'It's a bit boring looking,' I said, failing to hide my disappointment.

'But, Professor Lockwood, you of all people should know that hidden between the pages of these ledgers and journals are tales more fascinating than any stuffed dodo or the skeleton of the Irish Giant.'

'There *are* no stuffed dodos,' I corrected him.

'Picky,' Mark declared.

When I'd lived in London, I'd been a regular visitor to the Natural History Museum and was friends with a member of staff. The dodo on display was a replica, largely based on a painting which might not even have been painted from life. Its feathers were actually taken from a swan on the Thames.

'Now take a seat at that table.' Mark went to a shelf and removed a box. Inside was a small leather book, well-worn but otherwise in good condition. A couple of other small objects were in protective wrapping or slotted into foam, but I focused on the book.

'Aren't we meant to wear gloves?' I asked.

'These days, the view is that so long as you have clean hands washed with soap and water, it's fine. Gloves can be just as dirty,

81

and don't allow as much dexterity. You're more likely to rip pages in gloves because you can't feel the paper.'

'Shouldn't we have someone with us, a curator?'

Mark shook his head. 'I've had training, and I've now been in here often enough with one of them that they let me sign the keys out unaccompanied. You, on the other hand… well, it's questionable whether having you with me is allowed, so it's probably better that you don't broadcast this visit.'

'My lips are sealed. So tell me about this.'

'This is the diary of Mary Ollerenshaw, a maid at the time that Dwin Lee was killed. Her descendants likely donated this to the house when they found it. It's in fantastic condition.'

I was hesitant to do so much as open the cover.

'Go on, it won't bite. I'm going to see what else there is; I'm hoping there's a record of visitors or mail, or something. I also want to figure out if maybe some of the people we've come across worked here at the house.'

I turned some of the pages as he talked. The paper was thin and starting to go brown, the writing childish and spidery.

'Do you think Dwin's death could have a link to the house?'

'No idea. I was thinking that we might find out a bit more about the individuals concerned, rather than a straight link. That would be too good to be true.'

While Mark carefully examined the contents of box files, looked things up online with his phone and made notes, I read Mary's diary. At first, I felt as if I was intruding. It was her personal diary and she no doubt intended it to be for her eyes only. But before long, I got caught up in the day-to-day gossip, and even the lists of the jobs that she'd been given to do on certain days were a fascinating glimpse into her life.

She didn't shy away from complaining about other people's decisions.

'"*Mrs Banks hired a new maid, she is too short. I know I will just be* called on to do extra work she cannot manage. I reckon she is related to Mrs Banks, they are way too familiar." What's that about?' I asked Mark. 'What's wrong with being short?'

He laughed. 'They wanted maids who could clean high up, or reach across wide tables and put things away on high shelves, so height was a factor they'd take into account. You wouldn't stand a chance.'

'Unless I was related to Mrs Banks, by the sounds of things.' I guessed that she was the housekeeper. 'Listen to this: "Bert has got himself mixed up with a girl, he says it is love and they intend to marry. That is his career over with. I wonder how long he will last here after they marry." Why would getting married be the end of his career? I thought it was women who often had to stop working once they got hitched?'

'Bert was a butler here. It was just the nature of the job that their loyalty was expected to be 100% to their master. If you're married, that loyalty becomes divided. Plus once they had children, which was assumed would come next, they were less employable. No one wanted to take on a butler with a wife and children; accommodating them became harder. A lot of butlers knew that their future was one of single-minded loyalty, and then they became so ingrained in that life that they just couldn't imagine themselves existing outside in the "real" world.'

I read on. Mary was a typical teenager in many ways, complaining about the other staff and who wasn't pulling their weight. I could see why Mark said she had a thing for George Henry. There were comments about his striking eyes, how he glanced at her and smiled when she stepped out of his way in a corridor. How smart he'd looked after a recent haircut. Each one innocent on its own, but when they were regularly dotted about the diary entries, it was easy to see the young girl was besotted with what sounded like a handsome young man.

Once I got about halfway through, there was finally the

mention of a name that made me sit up straight and pay attention.

I read the extract to Mark. '"*Spent some of my day off with Catherine. We talked about our plans for Christmas and if the Fitzwilliam-Scotts will have a party for the estate staff again. She would like a new dress, but her father cannot afford it. She told me she is in love. She would not say who with except that he behaves like a gentleman and can offer her a comfortable future, he has also offered to pay off her father's debts.*" Do you think that's Catherine Austin?'

'Yes. Keep going, see if you can find more.'

It wasn't long until I read out, '"*Catherine says her father had to throw out some of the estate workers for fighting. They were drunk and he threatened to tell the Duke about their behaviour. Of course he will not, it happens all the time.*" I thought you said the pub had a reputation for being quiet?'

'I guess it's all relative. Turfing a couple of men out after a scuffle is different to a full-blown riot,' Mark said. 'Take some photos of the relevant pages, we can look at them in more detail later.'

I nodded, but read on.

'You've caught it, haven't you?' Mark said with a satisfied smile.

'What?'

'The bug. It's fun, isn't it? You get sucked in.' He was right, but I didn't reply to that comment as I had found something else.

'There's more on the Duke's son. Mary really was taken with him. The way she writes, I think she's rather jealous of those who get to work anywhere near him. Have you found much more?'

He shook his head.

'Bit of a bust here, I'm afraid. I'll chat to one of the curators on Monday and see if they can point me in the direction of anything. All I've been able to prove is that George was quite the spender. It looks like he even ordered his own beer. Not surprising, we know he liked a party. I'm getting hungry, should we go and get lunch?'

As soon as he said it, I realised I was starving. We packed away our notebooks and carefully returned the journal to the shelf, but I wanted to come back and read more. Mark had been right: the room might look a bit boring, but once you got stuck in, there really were treasures between the pages.

CHAPTER 13

I'd decided to risk being grabbed by my staff and buy lunch at the Stables Café. If I was honest, I slightly neglected this café. Out in the stable block so visitors didn't have to buy a ticket to reach it, it sold simple, hearty food: sandwiches, hot rolls and soup. The polished concrete floor could easily contend with muddy boots and on the walls we'd displayed large photographs taken throughout the gardens and estate.

We were surrounded by dog walkers and families who had dragged their children out to get some fresh air. I grabbed us a couple of sausage butties, slathering mine in tomato ketchup and Mark's in brown sauce, along with two coffees. We chose to sit away from the visitors, side by side on a stone step on the far side of the courtyard.

The courtyard was an enormous space, bigger than the original house had been, and had held eighty horses, its own blacksmith and accommodation for all the staff involved with the care of the animals. These days, the stables held a café, a gift shop, a small exhibition space and areas used for storage. Above them were a couple of offices and small apartments, one of which was lived in by Father Craig. I guessed the one with the glowing neon Nativity scene in the window was his.

We pulled up our collars and sat close together, trying to keep warm. The breeze was refreshing, so I didn't mind the cold that accompanied it.

'Hello, you two.' A tall, slim good-looking man with two black Labradors stopped in front of us. 'Hiding from the masses? Very wise.'

Alexander Fitzwilliam-Scott, the 12th Duke of Ravensbury, and also the Viscount Earlfield and Baron Hadfield, was an elegant man with striking features, a nose that some might describe as Roman and perfect posture that made me instinctively pull my shoulders back. He looked just the part of the country gentleman in his corduroy trousers and waxed jacket. The dogs strained on the leads to get closer to our sausages, but the Duke told them to sit and they obeyed, their noses wiggling in the air, trying to suck in as much of the meaty aroma as possible.

Mark and I both started to stand, but the Duke waved us back down. He wasn't one for formality, unless the occasion particularly called for it.

'It's good to see you both taking a break. You need to escape the office – or kitchen – occasionally, maintain your sanity.'

'We've actually been doing some research,' I said. 'Mark took me into the conservation stores.'

I felt Mark's foot knock against mine. Oops! I wasn't meant to tell anyone.

'I haven't been in there for years. Find anything interesting?'

I realised that the Duke had no idea who was and wasn't allowed in the storerooms so I carried on, like an excited child who'd enjoyed their day at school.

'I was reading the diary of one of the servants, it was fascinating. Everything she had to do. It was quite funny, really, she had a bit of a crush on one of the family: George Henry.'

I could tell I'd caught the Duke's attention.

'George Henry, eh? I assume you mean the son of the 8th – now there's a man with an abundance of skeletons in his closet.'

'Funny you should say that, we're looking into the skeleton that was found at the Black Swan.'

The Duke laughed. 'Of course you are, Sophie, that doesn't surprise me in the slightest.' He stopped and the smile left his face. 'Do you think that George might have had something to do with it?'

I looked over at Mark. 'Not necessarily, but he does appear to have a link with the pub. There's no reason there's any connection to Dwin.'

'Who's Dwin?' the Duke asked.

'Dwin Lee, the skeleton. At least we're about 99% sure it's him.'

The Duke sighed. 'Are you both due back at work or do you have time for a bit of storytelling? We don't talk all that much about George, but you might be interested.'

'Yes, yes, absolutely.' We shot up and shoved what was left of our butties in our mouths. The Duke looked a little surprised, but then nothing that we'd just done was the typical way to behave in front of a peer of the realm.

'Come on, we'll go to the library. It's much warmer in there.'

The Duke led us up a stone staircase that I was familiar with and let us into his private library.

'Make yourselves at home, I'll just take the dogs down.' He looked at the carpet and the muddy paw prints. 'Should have taken them in the other way. Oh well.'

He left the room, and Mark and I stood and stared at one another. It was like being shown into the inner sanctum, the various shades of dark red fabric and brown wooden shelves and detailing closing in around us. I'd assumed I'd never be allowed back after falling asleep in here one evening. Fortunately, the Duke has a sense of humour and, hopefully, a short memory.

He returned a few minutes later to find us still standing.

'Sit, sit, for heaven's sake, don't stand on ceremony. I've asked for some warm drinks to be brought up. Come on.' He directed us to the sofa, then he sat in an armchair by the side of the fireplace. His perfectly tailored trousers rose just enough to uncover some rather colourful socks, but not enough to reveal bare leg.

The Duke looked around. 'This is my favourite room in the winter. It's extremely – what's the word? Cosy, I suppose you might say. But then you'd know about how relaxing this room can be, Sophie.'

Okay, so he didn't have a short memory. He smiled.

'Sorry, couldn't resist. But there is a chaise longue over there if you get tired.' Mark and I laughed. 'Anyway, to the point. You know I've never been particularly coy about the more interesting members of my family. Quite frankly, it's a lot better that I talk about them than an ill-meaning journalist, plus the visitors love it, and I'm not averse to a bit of gossip myself. Over the centuries, there's probably been more affairs and illegitimate children in the family than even I'm aware of. I imagine a few of my ancestors deserved the title "crook", too, although perhaps it's best I don't know about those.

'But George Henry Fitzwilliam-Scott, the youngest son of the 8th Duke, really was a personality. He'd make a damned good film character, although he certainly wouldn't be a hero figure.' The Duke paused as a smartly dressed young man appeared with three mugs on a tray. They looked distinctly like hot chocolate and I was sure I could see marshmallows bobbing on the top of the steaming liquid. I had to stop myself squeaking with delight.

After thanking the young man, the Duke continued. 'George was a little wayward, never really found his path in life. You've heard of the idea of an heir and a spare?' We both nodded. It had been more commonly used in relation to monarchs. The reigning monarch had once needed a son to guarantee the family's place on the throne. In centuries gone by, it was not uncommon for children to die young, or if they lived a little longer, to die on the battlefield. It was, therefore, useful to have a second son who could take over as monarch and not have the crown move to another branch of the family, or a different family entirely, if the first son and heir were to die. Many people forget that Henry VIII, for example, was actually the 'spare', his older brother Arthur originally being next in line until he died at only sixteen years of age.

'George wasn't even the spare, he was the spare's spare. He was restless and ultimately quite the playboy. Money trickled through his fingers like it was water; he was forever chasing the ladies, regardless of their social status. Drank too much and generally got away with murder – not literally, of course.

'He was, I'm afraid, his mother's favourite so was never really punished for anything he got up to. I have no doubt that he left a number of children scattered around Derbyshire and I know for a fact that his parents provided an annuity to the child of one servant he got pregnant. If they'd been aware of more, and I'm sure there were more, they would have done the same thing for those children, too. They were desperate to marry him off, but he wasn't keen to give up the playboy lifestyle he had become accustomed to.

'Well, his father eventually threatened to cut off all financial support unless he married and he was introduced to Lady Mary Boyle. His reputation was well known, but her family was desperate to move in slightly better circles and was prepared to sacrifice their daughter's happiness, if necessary, in order for her to marry into our family. She was an attractive young thing and, as many women did, fell for him almost immediately. They were introduced at a party – a Christmas party, I think, down in London – and about three months later, were married.

'They moved to London where his philandering continued.

Roughly a year later, he started an affair with the wife of a prominent politician. Now there was no evidence, but the feeling was that it was this affair that led to his death less than a year afterwards. He was found beaten to death in an alley, apparently the victim of a theft. The word on the street was that it was carried out at the request of the politician, but if that's true, the men he hired to carry it out were very good and left behind no clues.'

'What happened to George's wife?' I asked. I felt sorry for her.

'She did rather well, by all accounts. Marrying into the family had the desired effect and she was able to socialise with some important people, one of whom fell in love with her. Her second husband was a very rich widower who treated her well. She didn't have any children of her own, but was close to her stepchildren.'

'How come we don't know about all of this?' Mark looked genuinely curious. 'As you say yourself, you're known for inviting people to examine your cupboards for skeletons; you certainly don't hide them.'

'There is a world of difference between hiding and just neglecting to mention. My feeling is that people are so used to us telling the stories ourselves, they assume there is nothing left to look for. Rather useful, really.'

'And if this gets out?' I asked.

'So be it. I'm not ashamed; it's the reality of the past. If I have to talk about it, I will.' He smiled his usual charming smile. 'Now then, somewhere I have...' He walked over to a bookcase and pulled out a large book. Back in his seat, he opened it up on his knee and turned the pages of what turned out to be a photo album. 'Here we are.' He pulled out a photograph and handed it to Mark, whose eyes lit up.

'Whoa! He's a looker. Oh, I'm sorry.'

The Duke laughed. 'That's quite alright. He was a very handsome man, although I am a little more used to the ladies responding in that manner. If you promise to look after it and return it when you're done, you can borrow it. It was taken at the party I mentioned, the night he met his wife.'

Mark handed me the photo. I understood his response. George was extremely good-looking.

'Would he have ever had a reason to visit the pub?' I asked. 'The Black Swan... well, it was the Plough in those days.'

'Possibly. I go a couple of times a year, show my support for charity events, that sort of thing. The Duchess, of course, designed the interior of the guest rooms, flexing her creative muscles. It would have been much more rough and ready in the late 19th century, but I find it easy to imagine that George would have decided it would be a lark to go and have a drink with the locals once in a blue moon. Based on what I know of him, I can picture him being rather patronising, but the locals would probably have had their beer paid for and put up with him. We bought the land and the pub around then, but I'm pretty sure it was after George's time.'

I'd been wary of asking the Duke directly for information on his ancestor, but I should have known he'd be happy to talk. I couldn't think of anything else to ask him for the time being and didn't want to overstay our welcome. We might need him again in the future.

'Thank you, this has been really interesting. We should leave you to it.'

'And you two should enjoy your weekend. Your commitment is commendable, but I'm sure there is something fun you could be doing this close to Christmas.'

Mark smiled. 'We can think of a few things, thank you.'

We left the warmth of the library and exchanged it for chilly air that made us pull our jackets tightly around us, but at least the mist had long since lifted. I looked at my watch: we hadn't been with the Duke for as long as I'd thought. It was only two o'clock.

'Right then, I'm off home. We can catch up about all this tonight. You walking to your car?' Mark asked.

'No, there's plenty of time and I fancy a walk. I'm going to head over to the church.'

'Seriously? It's freezing.'

'It won't be once I get moving, and I ought to get a bit of exercise so I can justify indulging later.'

'Better you than me. Don't get lost; Bill makes a particularly spectacular Lancashire hotpot, and we *will* eat it all without you.'

I kissed him on the cheek and set off into the gardens.

CHAPTER 14

$\mathcal{I}$ had been shown a little-known path that would take me out of the formal gardens into the wider estate. It was a good job it was little-known and well-hidden, otherwise we'd have had visitors trying to avoid paying for the ticket needed to enter the gardens.

There wasn't the riot of colour found in the spring and summer, but the numerous shades of green gave the vast gardens depth and variety. Dotted around were tall, ghostly white shapes. Hovering above bushes and walls, they watched over me from the sides of the paths and the middle of flowerbeds, looking like the white sheet ghosts that children drew, only they didn't have holes for eyes. They did, however, have ropes around them, as though the ghosts had been kidnapped and put on display.

Of course, the gardens weren't haunted by an insane number of apparitions. Rather, all the statues had been wrapped with protective white covers secured with ropes for the winter, avoiding the damage that came with frosts. But the effect was eerie and often elicited a second glance.

One statue was being worked on; it seemed the rope had come loose and the cover had been flapping around, about to break free. Two people in matching bottle-green jackets were tidying it up, and as I got closer, I recognised one as Esther Marsh, the volunteer who had given a talk on poisonous plants.

'Need any help?' I called out.

'No thanks, we've got it.' The male gardener tied the rope off and acknowledged me with a slight wave. 'We're done here. Time to get a brew, I reckon.'

'Esther…' I called. I wanted the chance to talk to her about the chapel volunteers.

'You go ahead, Rob, I'll catch up with you in the break room.' She turned to me as she kept the breeze from blowing her steel grey hair into her face. 'Can we make it quick? It's too cold to stand here chatting.'

From her tone, I knew I'd picked a bad time.

'Sure. We didn't get much of a chance to talk last time I saw you. I was wondering how well you knew the other three who were poisoned. Not Harriet, the others.'

She sighed as though she was bored of the subject. 'You don't know the volunteers well, do you?'

I shook my head. 'Not at all. Well, Harriet, but everyone knows her.'

'Someone will tell you soon enough. My husband was Kenneth's business partner. Kenneth royally screwed him over, so he's not in my good books. If he was capable of betraying my husband, then I would strongly suspect there are others who would happily see him suffer.'

'What do you mean, "screwed him over"?'

'This doesn't mean I did it, you know?'

I couldn't tell whether she was scared or angry. 'No, of course not, I just want to get an idea of what happened, help Craig get this sorted as quickly as possible. I'm not here to point fingers.'

That was a lie; I absolutely wanted to know who'd done it and point my finger squarely at them. No wonder she'd avoided the question when I last saw her in the house.

'They ran a small accounting firm together. The two of them, a couple of bookkeepers, a payroll manager. They had it all planned out: when they'd retire, what they'd do with the business. But Kenneth decided he wanted out early. Gave almost no notice. Of course, most of Kenneth's clients went elsewhere, and work they'd shared landed on my husband's desk. Kenneth wanted buying out, which drained our savings.

'Now my husband works every hour God sends trying to keep the business going long enough to be able to make back some of the savings we had to give up. I retired from my own career long ago, but now I go in three days a week to help. Coming here and helping in the gardens goes some way to keeping me sane. I've every reason to want him to suffer, but I didn't do it. He's not worth the energy.'

I could see the colour rising in her cheeks and her shoulders tensing as she talked. Her voice was steady, but she couldn't hide all of her body's reactions. She was angry, really angry. She had more than enough reason to want to make Kenneth very uncomfortable for a night.

'Anything else?' she asked sharply.

'No,' I replied. 'Thank you.'

I watched as she stomped up the path towards the house. Was she trying to distract me by telling me all this, hoping that I'd assume she couldn't possibly have done it because she so easily admitted to the link? If so, she'd just failed. She'd added herself to my list of suspects a lot earlier in the game.

It was only a twenty-minute walk to St Anne's Church, which was within the boundaries of the estate and, in years gone by, would have been where the Charleton House staff and estate workers would have worshipped. The chapel inside the house had been reserved for family members only; that had changed now and it had a small but active congregation from around the area who could come in for services without paying for a ticket. Craig also carried out services in St Anne's church and was responsible for its general upkeep.

It was a sweet little place made of local limestone, portions of it dressed in gritstone which added a rough and hardened appearance to the building, making it look like it had been there forever, able to withstand anything that the elements or humans threw at it. It had a round arched doorway with a sounding hole above it and a little slit window to either side. The idea was that the hole would allow the sound of the congregation at song to spread far and wide. Craig had told me that in practice, it was almost entirely decorative and had long since been filled in. I was a little disappointed; I'd liked the idea of a rudimentary speaker system blasting the hymns across the rolling hills.

A small graveyard surrounded the church within a dry stone wall, moss covering many of the gravestones. I didn't think it would take long for me to find the gravestone of Catherine Austin, but after half an hour, I was starting to get cold and dispirited.

'Sophie?' Craig had appeared around the side of the church. 'What are you doing here?'

'Hey. I'm looking for Catherine Austin's grave.'

'It's over here, I just walked past it.' Craig took long strides and headed for the far corner near the wall. 'Here we are: *Catherine Austin, 1863–1885, and Edwin "Dwin" Austin, her son.*'

It was a simple grey slab, nothing fancy at all, no mention of them being loved. No mention of Catherine being a beloved daughter. It all seemed so very sad.

I looked around. 'Where's her father's grave? William?'

'Hmm, that doesn't ring any bells. It's not a big graveyard and I've studied the records a few times, I don't think I've ever come across him.'

There was something that stood out: Catherine's child had been called Edwin. Either she had lived long enough to name the child, or she must have decided before the birth what she would call it if it was a boy, and she had chosen Edwin, and the moniker 'Dwin'. That can't have been a coincidence, surely? I thought back to the chapter in the local mysteries and myths book about Dwin's disappearance. He had been described as a kind man who was good with children, an unofficial uncle to many. If Catherine had known him, spent time with him and was fond of him, then perhaps she had planned to name her child after him. It didn't say much for her father if she would name her child after an old local man rather than its grandfather.

I imagined the delight on old Dwin's face at being told of this, had he lived. Of how he might have played with the child and been a positive influence. Next time, I'd remember to bring flowers.

I must have looked a bit downhearted as Craig put his hand on my shoulder and gave it a squeeze.

'Come on, it's getting cold. Do you want a lift home?'

'No, thank you. My car's back up at the house and I'd like to walk up there, clear my head.'

'Okay. I'll see you at seven. Can I bring anything?'

'Beer, if that's what you're drinking, and one of your fantastic hugs.'

'You're on.'

He walked me as far as the church door, and then went inside. I couldn't wait to entertain my friends later, but first I wanted to be alone for a while. I wanted to spend some time with a few ghosts and see if what I was learning about them was starting to add up. That, and I still needed to burn off a lot more calories before the evening of overindulgence we had planned.

CHAPTER 15

Once I'd made it home, I cleaned the cottage from top to bottom, irritating Pumpkin no end. She hated the vacuum cleaner with a passion and hid under the bed until she was certain it was back in the cupboard beneath the stairs. I really should have decorated the Christmas tree, but I had procrastinated so much that the decorations were still in the box and the tree was lopsided in the corner of the sitting room, serving as a scratching post for Pumpkin. If anyone complained, they could do it for me.

There was something else I wanted to do before my guests arrived. I pulled up a chair and sat at the kitchen table, took a deep breath and ripped open the Christmas card I'd been carrying around with me.

On the front was an illustration of a snow-covered London with St Paul's Cathedral in the background. So far, so harmless. I stared at it for a moment, not really taking the image in. With another deep breath, I opened it and scanned the familiar handwriting. Prepared for a request to see me or a long, heartfelt apology, I was oddly disappointed. Instead the words were brief and simple.

'To Sophie, with fond memories of Christmas past. I hope the New Year is as wonderful as you deserve. With love, Adam.'

Should I make an attempt to read between the lines? Did he hope that the New Year would see him back in my life, or was it all really as simple as it looked? I couldn't ponder it for long as I heard voices and the stamping of feet on my mat.

I tossed the card on a pile of unopened mail. I'd come back to it later.

'Coo-eee, your guests of honour are here.' I'd left the door on the latch so everyone could let themselves in. 'Where's that tabby coloured rat of yours? Hope you've kicked her out for the night.'

'Mark!' Bill sounded horrified. 'Sorry, Soph, but you know what he's like. You shouldn't invite him. Where do you want this?'

Bill was carrying a large casserole dish and I led him to the oven.

'Stick it in there, it'll keep it warm until everyone is here.' He closed the oven door, then gave me one of his bone-crushing hugs. Although not as fit as he'd been in his professional rugby days, he had maintained the bulk and some of the strength.

'Sophie, come in here. Bill, you won't believe this.' I followed the direction of Mark's voice into the sitting room. I knew what he was going to say. 'It's Christmas, woman. What were you planning on doing? Using this as scented firewood? It's all it will be good for if you don't put it in some water.'

Bill looked at me and shook his head. 'Cruelty to trees, Miss Lockwood, cruelty to trees. Leave this to me.'

While I poured drinks, Bill put the tree in the holder and added water. I joined them and found Mark rooting through the box of decorations.

'Where's your fairy?'

I gave him a lopsided grin. 'Do you really want me to answer that?'

I heard Bill quietly snigger. Mark looked at him.

'If *someone* had allowed me to retain my beautifully gilded moustache, then I would have been perfect for the role.'

'Is this the latest party game? "Decorate the tree because the host was too lazy to do it herself"?'

I hadn't heard Joyce come in.

'That's not a bad idea,' I replied. She handed me two bottles of champagne.

'Chilled and ready to pop.' Joyce had opted for tiger-print leggings. Or I thought they were tiger print; they could have been any big cat. Her cream sweater had tiny reindeers all over it. Her hair was a little more relaxed than usual and had gone from mound of blonde to a sort of fountain-like spout. I wasn't sure what she was trying achieve and was too afraid to ask.

'New wig?' asked Mark, clearly braver than I. I let the cork fly out of one of the bottles; it was perfect timing and distracted Joyce enough to stop her from stabbing him with the decoration she was adding to the tree. I didn't need a third crime to investigate.

'Starting without me?' Craig bounded in. 'Sorry I'm late. Harriet wanted a word, and as you can imagine, one of her words equates to ten of everyone else's.'

'Stop talking and drink,' I ordered, filling his glass.

'Happy Christmas!' we cheered in chorus. Bill and Mark then went to the kitchen to dish out bowls of Lancashire hotpot, and Craig helped Joyce finish decorating the tree while I added a log to the fire.

'It's nice to see some colour in this ice box of a room, even if it is temporary,' Joyce commented. I couldn't entirely disagree; I had slightly overdone it with the white walls and cream sofa. Joyce had long threatened to take me shopping, but I'd managed to dodge it so far. I couldn't bear the thought of the animal print cushions or mustard yellow sofa she'd probably talk me into buying.

I could smell Bill's creation before he and Mark reappeared, carrying bowls for everyone. A northern classic, Lancashire hotpot is a wonderfully warming winter stew. It probably started out as a jumble of ingredients, but these days lamb is usually the main one. Kidneys and onions were in there and the gravy was nice and thick. There was a layer of potatoes at the bottom, and on the very top. The trick was making the top layer not too crispy and not too soft. Bill had got it just right.

As we ate, Mark and I filled everyone in on our research. Joyce was particularly taken with our description of George Henry Fitzwilliam-Scott.

'Shame I wasn't around back then, he sounds like he needed a more mature woman to guide him through life.'

'It's an interesting point you make about the child's name,' Craig said. 'I'd assume the same thing you did, that Dwin had a positive influence on Catherine.'

'So who would want to kill such a sweet man?' asked Bill as he topped up everyone's glasses, popped the cap off a beer for Craig, and then made himself comfortable on the floor in front of the fire. 'He doesn't sound like he'd hurt a fly.'

'You think the Duke's son is behind it, don't you?' said Joyce, peering at me through suspicious half-closed eyes.

'I'm not sure. Not long after Dwin disappeared, a man, Michael Hall, was hung for the murder of someone else. Hall was at the pub the day of the brawl. I wonder if Dwin stopped him trying to steal from the pub or angered him in some way. If he was quick thinking, Hall could have pushed him into the cellar and hidden him under a load of rubble while the landlord was dealing with the brawl going on outside. In all the noise and chaos, Hall wouldn't have been missed for the period of time it took to conceal the body.'

Mark looked doubtful.

'You don't agree?' I asked him.

'It's one possibility. But George was a man who got what he wanted, especially when it came to women – remember what

Mary said about Catherine and her admirer. He was a gentleman who could afford to pay off her father's debts. The Duke told us today that George would go after women regardless of their social status, and Catherine was way below him. I wonder if he wanted Catherine, and Dwin tried to protect her? After all, it would be an enormous scandal: an unmarried woman getting pregnant by someone who couldn't or wouldn't marry her. Some families would try and find someone who could be convinced to marry their pregnant daughter in order to avoid the scandal, as getting married when pregnant wasn't quite such a big deal, but to remain unmarried? That could have destroyed her, and if she was blinded by love, then maybe Dwin stepped in to protect the girl he cared about and tried to warn George off.'

'We don't even know if George was attracted to her. We don't have any references to them being together.'

'Agreed, but we know he had dealings with her father, so the chances are he met her when they were sorting out the money.'

'None of this sounds very exciting.' Joyce was gathering up the bowls. 'I prefer the cases where I have to be prepared to tackle someone at a moment's notice.' She took on a kung fu pose and dropped all the spoons.

Craig laughed. 'Very dynamic.'

I followed Joyce out, picking up the dropped spoons on the way.

'Leave them on the side, I'll sort it out later.'

Before I could stop her, she had picked up the Christmas card I'd dumped on the side.

'Who is Adam, and why is he fondly thinking of past Christmases together?' It was remarkable just how high she could raise her eyebrows. 'What are you not telling me, young lady? Is this why Joe's new romance isn't quite the concern I'd expected it to be?'

'It's nothing,' I said, taking the card off her and stashing it under a newspaper. 'Just an old friend.'

'Then why are you hiding it when I've already seen it?'

'No reason, it's just not important.'

'That's the biggest load of codswallop I've heard all day.' She picked up the envelope beside the card and examined the postmark. 'Is he… is he your fiancé? The one who was arrested for stealing money from the restaurant you both worked at?'

'*Ex*-fiancé,' I said firmly. 'Yes, alright. It's him.'

'And…?'

'And nothing. It would have been easy enough for him to find out that I was back up here and working at Charleton, and I have no intention of replying.'

'I hope not. I'm still holding out for you and Joe. I know I've told you you're fine on your own and don't need a man, but come on, you'd make the most adorable couple.'

'There's a chocolate cake under that cover, and ice cream in the freezer. I'll get clean bowls and spoons.'

'Stop trying to change the subject.'

I ignored her, but I couldn't help but think of the wonderful Christmas dinners Adam had cooked, how he made stuffing that was packed with flavour and bread sauce that was the perfect consistency.

Stop it, I told myself. *You've moved on.* There was no escaping the fact that I was a sucker for the romance of Christmas, and the relationship had ended on decidedly unromantic terms. That was what I needed to remember.

'Come on. Let's feed the boys before they start complaining, but don't think this conversation is over, young lady.'

It wasn't long before Craig was lounging on the floor. After three pieces of cake, he'd concluded he was spending the night there, incapable of getting up. I was surprised; he looked like a man to whom a couple of slices of cake was a starter.

I'd been telling my guests excitedly about the fascinating

insight into the life of servants I'd been discovering in the Charleton House stores.

'Mary comes across as quite a gutsy girl. She doesn't seem to miss much and I can imagine her standing up for herself. She'd make a great character in a television drama.'

'But was the diary helpful?' Bill asked.

'Very. It gave me a better sense of some of the people we're dealing with, and she knew Catherine and William. I didn't have time to read it all; I want to go back, or maybe you can, Mark?'

'If I get time. I have quite a few tours booked in this week. We get private groups who book a tour, then go for lunch and get sloshed on the company credit card. There's also a postgrad student I want to talk to who has been researching the servants at Charleton and making a database of all the employees, as far back as records allow. I'm hoping she can throw some light on a few things.'

Unnoticed, Pumpkin had joined us and was now head-butting Joyce's leg. Joyce responded to the demand and gave her a long, indulgent stroke.

'Cute kitty, where have you been all night?'

'Terrorising the neighbourhood, I imagine,' said Mark. Pumpkin jumped up on Joyce's lap.

'She likes me!' Joyce declared triumphantly, looking at Mark. 'She clearly has good taste.'

'She's mistaking your leggings for an ancestor, and you appear to use the same nail technician.' I was grateful for Mark's sake that, with Pumpkin's large bulk on her knee, Joyce was unable to get up and do him any harm.

'How are you feeling about next week?' Craig grinned at me. It took me a minute to realise what he was talking about. I scowled at him.

'No comment.'

'You'll be the highlight of the event. I need some new blood giving readings and you'll enjoy it, I know it. Christmas services in that chapel can't be anything other than memorable and everyone I've spoken to is so excited that you're taking part.'

'Yeah, about that,' I grumbled, 'even Harnby knows. I never actually said yes.'

'In your heart you did,' said Craig before hiding behind his beer glass.

'Speaking of the police, are we not meant to mention this evening to Joe as he wasn't invited?' asked Joyce.

'He was invited,' I replied, 'but he's out with Ellie. I suppose I could have invited her too. Now I feel bad.'

'Don't be so soft,' snapped Joyce as she scratched behind Pumpkin's ears. 'You did the right thing, it's too early for you to be inviting them around as a couple.'

She was still making it sound as though Joe and I had been together.

'Who wants coffee?' I leapt up, keen to change the subject. The murmur of approval at the idea had me heading into the kitchen to grind beans. I stopped and picked up Adam's Christmas card as I walked past the counter. Since I had left London, I had been distracted by a new job and new friends, and a few dead bodies. I wondered if it was time to finally confront the past of the living variety.

CHAPTER 16

I couldn't remember the last time I had been to church on a Sunday. I was hard pressed to remember the last time I'd been to church for a service at all. Most of my friends in London had been married in registry offices, or in unusual locations like the Tower of London. One had even been married in a pod on the London Eye, although I wasn't a close enough friend to be with them as they circled up into the clouds. I'd joined them later for the reception on a barge on the River Thames.

Today I opted for jeans with a cable sweater and a long, warm black coat, topped up the coffee in my travel mug, and drove to Charleton House. The one thing I'd forgotten to do was check my watch, and I arrived late. I knew that I could sneak in the back but I hated the thought of providing any kind of distraction, so I grabbed an almond croissant from the Library Café, much to the surprise of my staff, and took a back route into Craig's office to wait.

I was kicking myself for being so tardy. I'd always been a believer in 'late is late, on time is late, early is on time'. I also hated making a grand entrance of any kind. In fact, I hated drawing attention to myself at all, which was why giving a reading at the Christmas service was freaking me out.

I sat in Craig's office and stewed over his assumption that I was going to do the reading. Mark should have been asked instead; he loves an audience. I was still feeling rather grumpy, when the door opened and a woman I recognised as Sian Feathers came in.

She jumped when she saw me. She was smartly dressed; her understated style was simple yet classy and distracted from her poor posture. Once I'd spotted it, I wanted to grab her by the shoulders and tell her to stand up straight.

'Oh, oh, I wasn't expecting... who are you? You look familiar.'

'Sophie Lockwood, Head of Catering. You're Sian, right? Feeling any better?'

'Am I what? Oh that, yes, thank you.'

'Father Craig is still delivering the service,' I told her, although from the tone she responded with, I really needn't have bothered.

'Yes, I know *that*. I'd be in there myself only my washing machine flooded the kitchen. I wanted to make sure I was here to catch...'

Kenneth, I thought.

Sian was quietly spoken; her annoyance and soft voice made her sound like an irritable mouse. She was carrying a rather large handbag and I wondered if she'd come in to leave Craig another of the increasingly creepy anonymous Christmas gifts. Not that the gifts were creepy, just the regularity. If that had been her plan, I quickly scuppered it.

'Do you have a moment, Sian? They won't be finished for a little while and I'd really like to talk to you. Please sit.' I tried to make it as much like an instruction as possible without sounding rude. I was concerned I hadn't had enough coffee; I was starting to feel a little tetchy.

'Why? I...'

'Please, Sian.' I stood and pulled a chair in front of the desk. She reluctantly sat down.

'I really do hope you're feeling better after the other day. Do you have any idea who might have wanted to poison you?'

'Me?' She sounded shocked. 'Why me? It could have been any of us. Harriet in particular...'

'It wasn't Harriet they were targeting.' That was a lie. I had no idea who the target was, but I was getting tired of everyone assuming it was Harriet. I wasn't the biggest fan of the woman myself, but I was starting to feel sorry for her.

'But I haven't hurt anyone. Why would someone want to kill me?'

'Not kill you. Winterberries won't kill you, they'll just make you feel pretty rough for a while. So someone could just be annoyed by you, or want to send you a message. Is there anyone who you've had disagreements with, or who perhaps feels you have something they would like?'

'No, no one, and I really don't see what business this is of yours. I've already spoken to the police.'

I ignored her. 'How well do you get on with Verity?'

'Verity? Why would she want to poison me? We're friends. I mean, we have our disagreements from time to time, although...'

'Although what?'

'Well, she does make herself look rather ridiculous sometimes, the way she glues herself to Kenneth's side. I have wondered if she wishes I was around less – that way she could have him to herself.'

'But I thought you three were as thick as thieves.'

'Oh, we are, we are.' She sounded a little too keen to assert that idea. 'I just think... well...'

I wished she would get to the point.

'Verity is only recently widowed; it would be unseemly for her to dive into another relationship. I, on the other hand, am settled; Kenneth and I have much more in common. We've been friends the longest and just know each other so much better.'

'How do you know each other? From the chapel?'

'No, Kenneth and I met at a wine-tasting club and became friends there. We started to talk about faith and he suggested I join him for a service one day.'

'What about Verity?'

'She started attending services at the chapel not long after me.'

'How long ago was this?' She looked as if she was about to get up. 'Please, I won't ask any more questions after this.'

She let out an angry sigh. 'About twelve months ago.'

This time she did stand up, but our conversation was brought to a close anyway by the sound of the chapel congregation moving around, the voices turning into a cacophony of chatter as they started to leave, and the door between the chapel and the vestry opened and closed.

'I must go and find Kenneth; I know he'll be wondering where I was.'

Sian was out the door before I had time to thank her. She was like a heat-seeking missile. I wondered if I should feel sorry for Kenneth, too.

I thought about waiting for Craig, but I'd come to the service to see and hopefully talk to Sian and Verity. I'd ticked one of them off. It was time to find the other.

Verity Duff was easily recognisable by the red duffel coat she had taken to wearing in the colder weather. It made her look like Paddington Bear – Paddington Bear in high-heeled leather boots and thick eyeliner. She'd almost made it to the car park by the time I caught up with her.

'Verity, Verity, do you have a minute?'

'Oh, it's you. Sian said you'd been grilling her.' I doubted Sian had told Verity much else about our conversation. 'I have some-where to be.'

'Please, it will only take a minute.'

We had reached her car, a little red thing that matched her coat. I could see that the seats had been upholstered in matching black and red fabric. As I got closer, I saw that big plastic eyelashes had been attached above the front lights. It was effec-tive, but looked ridiculous.

'What?' She placed a hand on her hip. Her makeup was perfectly although heavily applied and I was hit by an overpow-ering aroma. It was like walking down the aisle in a department store and being targeted by a salesperson with the latest sickly perfume.

I didn't get a chance to ask a question.

'Look, I didn't poison anyone. I got sick, too, for heaven's sake. It was awful. I actually considered moving the TV into the bathroom at one point, I was spending so much time in there. Horrible, it was.'

'Is there anyone who might want to poison you?'

'What are you saying? I don't have enemies, I'm nice to every-one.' She spat out the words. 'If you want to point the finger at someone, point it at Harriet. She was the one banging on about the mulled wine and refusing to try a new recipe. She could have poisoned her own mulled wine that night, the perfect distraction, make me look bad, like I was trying to prove that her mulled wine was no good and we should go with my idea.'

I knew she wasn't serious, but she was so riled, I half expected steam to come out of her ears if she kept going like this.

'What about Sian?' I butted in.

'What about her? Good for a laugh, I suppose, but I do wish she'd leave Kenneth and I to it sometimes. We don't always need her hanging around like a spare wheel. Now if you'll excuse me, I have nothing more to say.'

She bundled herself into the car and, looking like an enormous ripe tomato, drove out of the car park. Or was it an enormous winterberry? What did Kenneth see in her? Perhaps he simply enjoyed female company. But she really wasn't keen to talk to me, and that always made me suspicious.

CHAPTER 17

*A*fter dealing with Sian and Verity, I craved the company of calmer, more sensible adults. Despite being considerably younger than Kenneth's fan club, my café assistant Chelsea met that description.

Chelsea Morris was a young woman who continued to impress me every day. She was only nineteen, and yet she juggled her job here as a café assistant with being her father's main carer since the death of her mother. She had struggled and her work had suffered, but once I'd found out about her home life, we'd done all we could to support her and she had blossomed.

She waved enthusiastically as I walked into the Library Café, and immediately turned towards the coffee machine. She had weaved red and gold wool into the plait in her hair and tied it off with a gold hairband.

'How was the morning service?' she asked as she steamed the milk for a latte. 'I saw you arrive and head that way.'

'I was late and didn't want to walk in while Father Craig was speaking. But I got to talk to the people I needed.'

'Did Harriet leave her teeth in you?' I had to laugh. Chelsea wasn't being vicious; she said it with a cheeky smile. 'I don't mean it; I quite like her. I'm not sure I'd want her as my grand-mother, but she'd make a fab godmother. You know, so I don't have to see her too much. I bet she protects her own like crazy. You don't think she did it, do you? Poisoned the others, I mean.'

'No, I don't, and I think you've hit the nail on the head. She's hugely protective of the chapel and everything to do with it. Other people see it as obstinacy, and maybe that's how it looks, but there's genuine good behind it. Even if some of the volunteers or congregation irritate her, they are still *chapel* volunteers or congregation and she's just as protective of them.'

'Yeah, plus this poisoning seems so silly. Dangerous, but silly. It's like a teenager trying to get attention: they start mucking around, getting into trouble. I was like that at school for a while. When Dad's illness was getting to me, I didn't know how to handle it and started being difficult. Nothing major, but I got detention a few times. Eventually a teacher I liked sat me down and started talking to me and it all came out. After that I got a bit more help and my grades improved. But it's hard to imagine Harriet behaving like a teenager. The bossy school matron, maybe.'

Chelsea just kept going up in my estimation. She was absolutely right. Harriet had never been high on my list of suspects, but Chelsea had just knocked her right off.

I called Mark as I walked back to my car, wanting to tell him about my morning. He picked up after only one ring.

'You must be psychic, I was about to call you,' were his first words.

'It's one of my many talents. You go first.'

'No, you.' This could have gone on all morning, so I started talking and told him I'd taken Harriet off the list of suspects, and about my conversations with Sian and Verity.

'Verity is a bit of a handful,' he confirmed. 'She came on one of my tours a couple of months back, almost knocked us unconscious with her perfume.' He made a gagging sound. 'She's very confident and I imagine she usually gets what she wants.'

I described how she was dressed when I saw her.

'You could be describing Joyce,' Mark said with mild amusement in his voice.

'No, Verity's like a cardboard cut-out. I don't think there's much beyond the surface. I don't mean that she's not bright, just that she's all show. Joyce – well, we both know there's more mystery there than we'll ever get to the bottom of. She's got more layers than an onion.'

'I don't think she'd like being compared to an onion.'

'An attractively scented leopard-print-wearing well-shod onion,' I clarified.

'Okay, so we're down to two jealous women, an ageing Casanova, and a wife with a grudge and a wealth of knowledge about poisonous plants,' he summarised.

'Information she conveniently shared with a lot of other people. Then, of course, there could be dozens of motives we know nothing about.' There was no response. 'Mark?'

'Sorry, just thinking. We have no idea who got into the vestry and added the berries, or left the cookies. Just like we have no idea who is leaving those gifts for Craig most mornings. Do you think the two things are connected?'

'Mark, you're brilliant.'

'I know. You can thank me later. One other thing, clear your diary for tomorrow morning. We're going into Manchester.'

'Why? Even if I am wildly distracted these days, I do have a number of cafés to pretend to run.'

He laughed a little too easily at that. 'We're off to meet Gretchen Dangerfield.'

'With a name like that, should I be worried? Downright scared?'

He laughed again. 'No, she's a PhD student from Manchester

University. She and a couple of others have been working on that database of all the servants who worked at Charleton House I told you about. Sadly we never got to meet when she was here over the summer, but I gave her a call on Friday. She's just messaged to say she could meet tomorrow, she has something that could be useful to us.'

I liked the sound of it, if only to meet someone with the name Dangerfield.

Harriet was loading boxes into the boot of her Mini Cooper. The car looked new. It was navy blue with racing stripes and was smarter and definitely cooler than any vehicle I'd ever owned. Once again, I surprised myself by being impressed with this increasingly impressive woman.

'Good afternoon, Harriet,' I called. She looked up.

'Ah, you.' She didn't sound pleased to see me.

'How are you?'

'As well as I was the last time you asked me that.'

So the standard pleasantries were a waste of time.

'How are the volunteers? Are they still talking about the poisoning or has it calmed down now?'

Harriet closed the boot of her car, sighed dramatically and put her hands on her hips. She seemed to have concluded that I wasn't going to just get in my car and drive off without some sort of exchange of meaningless – in her mind – chat.

'That lot will gossip about nothing else for a week, and then seem to have forgotten the subject ever existed. A ridiculous waste of time if you ask me. But I know you've been asking questions. Have you got any further than the police? They seem to be failing miserably, I haven't heard anything since the day they interviewed me.'

'I'm sure they're working hard.'

'Yes, well, they clearly need some help and I'm led to believe you are the person for that. You and those brash friends of yours. The one with the moustache and the blonde woman who looks like a stick of candyfloss.'

I laughed at that description. 'I'll do what I can. How's the party planning going?'

She made a tutting sound. 'We're having to meet again, we never finished the final details. I don't have a full list of those bringing cake and we never got to agree on the decorations. Esther dropped off examples of the table decorations, but we haven't chosen what we want yet.'

That confused me. 'Esther dropped them off? When?'

'During the meeting. She was with us before we started, but she'd forgotten to bring them so she went home and collected them.'

'Do the police know?'

'Of course they know she was there, I listed everyone who was with us, but cleared off before the meeting started.'

'But you told them she returned?'

'Of course I did... well, I think so. I must have done.' There was a flicker of uncertainty. 'I'm sure I did.' I was no longer sure who she was trying to convince. 'Well, I have no good reason to be standing in the cold talking to you. I should be home by now.' She tucked herself into the little car and left me open-mouthed as she set off with her wheels spinning and gravel flying everywhere. I wondered if there was something in the water around here. It seemed the older women got, the crazier they got.

It made me look forward to growing old at Charleton House.

117

It was at least twelve months since I'd last been into Manchester and I felt as if I was heading out on a school trip. I made sure my teams had everything they needed, which was probably guaranteed as what they needed was a break from me getting under their feet while they worked hard and I got distracted by the two cases I was trying to solve. They really were the most patient bunch of people. I just hoped it didn't backfire and I wouldn't discover that all my café assistants were running a shortbread smuggling cartel under my nose.

Right now, though, they could smuggle what they wanted; I was off to meet a female Indiana Jones, or so I imagined with a name like Gretchen Dangerfield. I was picturing a lot of khaki, bottle-bottom glasses, and an intense stare that could make me give away the location of my family's riches – if, indeed, any existed. She definitely worked in the wrong department. She should be in archaeology, not history, poring through the records of servants in an English stately home.

The journey was uneventful. We were joined by commuters who had missed earlier trains and students who were unfortunate enough to have a class before lunchtime on a Monday and didn't have time to sleep off hangovers. I watched out of the window as the scenery moved from damp countryside to suburbia, industrial estates, and then to Manchester city centre. I didn't make this journey very often and it was an enjoyable novelty.

It was a ten-minute walk from Manchester Oxford Road station to the university history department, past a jumble of modern glass buildings and Victorian houses that had been taken over by the university. Fast food joints, coffee shops and office supplies kept students fed, awake and with something to work on. Posters advertised club nights and new bars, and charity workers tried to stop us and get us to sign up to donate to their chosen campaign. This part of the city was awake, but only just.

The history department was based in a large, imposing red-brick building with a white portico entrance. We climbed the steps between two columns and under the portico that had gone grey with the muck in the city air: the building was just off Oxford Road, one of the busiest bus routes in Europe. Late-running students dashed past us and one nearly sent Mark flying.

'Sorry, mate,' the student shouted over his shoulder.

Mark had texted Gretchen as we walked from the station and she said she'd meet us, but as we stood in the middle of the heavily tiled entrance hall, we couldn't see her. I turned full circle, looking for the woman I imagined her to be. I had to remind myself she wouldn't be wearing a fedora or have a whip attached to her belt.

'Mark Boxer?' a hesitant voice asked. This must be her assistant. The slim woman had a tidy mousy-brown bob and matching brown eyes that darted back and forth between Mark and me.

'That's me, I'm here to see Gretchen Dangerfield.'

'Yes, hello, I'm Gretchen.' I nearly asked her if she was sure about that. 'Follow me, we can talk in my office. I have the kettle on.'

. . .

Gretchen's office was a small, plain space that she shared with two others. Apparently, they had already gone home for the Christmas break, but Gretchen lived here in Manchester full time. A few Christmas cards lined the windowsill, breaking up the view of a grey 1970s office block over the road. No romantic quads and courtyards for Gretchen.

'Thank you for travelling to see me. I wasn't due to head back to Charleton until the New Year, although I would have happily come out. It looks so lovely at Christmas.'

'Not a problem,' Mark replied. 'It's nice to get out for a couple of hours.'

'I don't know if you'll think it worth your while. I don't have a lot of information for you; I could have just told you over the phone.' I knew that Mark was really using this as an excuse to run a few additional errands while we were in the city, so it wouldn't have mattered if she had nothing useful to tell us, he'd still have come in.

Gretchen pulled up a database on her computer.

'We want to have a record of everyone who worked at Charleton House in one location that's easy to access by the public as well as the curators and staff on the estate, so I and another postgraduate student have been going through all the records.' She smiled shyly. 'It's been a wonderful summer, exploring the stores, talking to the Duke and Duchess, being able to wander the gardens on our lunch break. Quite idyllic, really. Now I'm tidying everything up and writing some articles.' She clicked through a series of screens as she talked. 'You told me about Mary Ollerenshaw. I scanned her diary and have photos of all the artefacts on here.'

'Artefacts?' I asked.

'Yes, the diary is in a box, right?' I nodded. 'Did you look at the other items in there?' Mark and I shook our heads.

'I didn't pay much attention,' he admitted. 'We were rather keen to get reading. We've read a lot of it, but what else can you tell us about her? It would be good if we could tell how reliable she was.'

When Gretchen smiled, her eyes seemed tiny. It was like talking to a little bird.

'That's a very good question. She was good at capturing gossip, but then she was a maid. Everyone was used to her coming and going; she was almost invisible, like a piece of furniture. People wouldn't have always registered her presence, so she could have overheard all sorts of things. She was fifteen when she entered service at the house and left in 1885 when she was eighteen.'

'Less than a year after Dwin was murdered,' I muttered. 'Didn't she want to progress? Wasn't she ambitious?'

'Perhaps, but she didn't behave like she did. She didn't leave of her own volition; she was fired.'

'Fired!' I exclaimed. 'I guess I haven't read far enough into her diary. Do we know what she did?'

Gretchen smiled and her little eyes appeared to sparkle. She might not have looked as if she could handle being chased through the Amazon, but she clearly had a love of discovery and following clues through history.

'She was stealing, and she doesn't write about it so you wouldn't have known. Those items in the box are some of the items she took. As far as we could tell, she mainly stole from George Henry Fitzwilliam-Scott. Based on her diary, she had quite a thing for him. She was still a young girl and was gathering trinkets. I'm sure that had she been able to, she would have taken a lock of his hair.'

So our assumption was right, she had been in love, or at least had a teenage crush on the handsome young man. I looked over at Mark, whose face was frozen with an expression that said, 'Yes, yes, tell me more.'

'Now there's something else that's interesting.' Her fingers flew across the keyboard as she typed something into the search box. 'When we spoke, Mark, and you told me the sorts of things you were thinking, you mentioned another name to me. A man who was hanged for murder not long after your man appears to have been murdered.'

'Yes, Michael Hall.'

'Well, his name appears in the records.' She scrolled down the page. 'He didn't work at the house for long, about six months. Here he is, Michael Hall, worked from July 1884 to January 1885. He was a general labourer. I don't have a record of his age or anything that could definitively say he was the same Michael Hall, but I would say the chances are high. The dates work, the proximity of the pub to the house. I don't know if it's all relevant or helpful, but I thought you might be interested.'

'Absolutely!' Mark exclaimed. 'That's fantastic. Thank you, Gretchen, this was definitely worth the journey.' She smiled, and then jumped as Mark patted her arm enthusiastically. 'You're a star.'

'Oh, oh, thank you,' she mumbled.

We could indeed have done this in a phone call, but it was so much more exciting to come and meet in person. It was like being on a mini adventure. We hadn't lifted a finger to find all this extra information, but being here with Gretchen made me feel a little more involved.

We thanked Gretchen profusely and told her to come and say hello the next time she was working at the house. Mark pretty much bounced down the steps of the building, then skipped ahead of me along the pavement, before skipping back.

'Isn't that fantastic? Right! Celebration coffee. I reckon your veins must be getting low on the stuff. I know where we'll go, follow me.'

The Manchester Museum is part of the university, and is one of those places that every schoolchild in the region gets taken to on a school trip at one time or another. The dinosaurs and Egyptian mummies are a winner for most kids, and they were with me. But right now, the only thing of interest was the enormous piece of carrot cake the museum café assistant was slicing for me. I could have taken it home and used it to stand on so I could reach the top shelf in my kitchen cupboards.

I ordered a bucket of coffee and sat down, ready to dissect our morning's findings with Mark.

'Okay,' Mark started, 'we need to look more closely at what Mary stole. Buttons and scraps of shaving soap or whatever they may be are hardly likely to help, but you never know. And then, what about Michael Hall? I know it's crossed our minds, briefly and uncomfortably, that George might have, shall we say, removed Dwin as an obstacle, but…'

'Maybe he paid someone to do it?' I interrupted. 'He would have had ample opportunity to come across Michael as he worked. Maybe he met him at the pub; maybe Michael had a reputation that George had heard about. If Michael bumped Dwin off and later tried to point the finger at George, who are people going to believe? Some general labourer with a reputation for violence, or a member of one of the most prominent families in the country? The Fitzwilliam-Scotts could have afforded the best solicitor money could buy. Michael wouldn't have stood a chance.'

'And he has already been placed at the pub on the day of the brawl – the day that Dwin was most likely killed,' Mark finished. I could feel the energy buzzing through me; I felt like bouncing up and down in my seat. But the thought of telling the Duke that his ancestor had basically hired a killer settled me down.

'We need to be really careful. We can't tell anyone about this until we're sure. It's hard enough gaining evidence for any of our theories, and at the end of all this, we still might just have a very strong idea of who killed Dwin. This is one idea we'd have to be able to back up with evidence, or we might see a different side to the Duke.'

Mark nodded. He looked as serious as I felt.

'You're right. The information about Mary is all on record so we're not saying anything new or controversial if we reveal that to anyone, but this possible link between George and Michael, we need to keep that to ourselves for now.' He picked up a fork and stuck it into my slice of cake. I didn't argue; it could have fed a family of four.

Once we'd demolished the carrot cake and I felt as if I had enough caffeine in my system to make it back to Charleton House, I said goodbye to Mark. According to his diary, he was carrying out research at Manchester Central Library; in reality, I knew he'd be attempting to max out his credit card in a book-shop. He was also likely to return home with a new pair of shoes, a couple of shirts and the glow of a man who had pampered himself in a barbers'. This was another secret that was safe with me, especially as it meant I knew he'd cover for me if I ever needed to carry out any 'research' of the baking kind.

It's called teamwork!

CHAPTER 19

'So how bad was the fall out between Kenneth and Esther's husband?' I asked Craig, who was working his way through his second piece of stollen. An afternoon snack he said he deserved after an hour with Harriet, who had her own ideas about how his filing should be organised.

'Bad enough that I don't think he and Esther have exchanged two words since Kenneth became part of the congregation. They won't go near each other.'

'Is the husband someone you think would use Esther's knowledge and take it out on Kenneth and whoever happened to be with him?' I asked.

'I doubt it. He's a pretty quiet chap. He clearly holds grudges, but he does it with a cold stare. I could probably count the conversations we've had on the fingers of one hand. He comes to services, arrives with minutes to spare, leaves immediately afterwards, and that's it. He's never here long enough to do anything else.'

'So why would Kenneth decide to come here if he knew that someone he's just had a major falling out with is already worshiping here? It almost sounds calculated.'

Craig shook his head. 'Kenneth's mother came here her whole life. Kenneth came as a young boy, but then dropped out of the habit and lost interest. He said he'd always planned to return when he retired and I believed him. We've not talked in any great depth about what happened with the business, but he has briefly acknowledged it with me and deeply regrets the difficulties he caused.'

'Not enough to change his plans or help out financially, though,' I added.

'Hmm, can't disagree with you on that. I don't think he's an inherently bad man, though. It does still leave us with Esther who, as I imagine you are about to suggest, has a strong enough motive to want to make Kenneth pay.'

I stole the last piece of stollen off his plate. It had been staring at me for too long.

'Oi!'

'Forgive me, Father, for I have sinned.'

'Fairly often, I imagine. You owe me one.' He picked up his napkin and wiped off the icing sugar that had coated his top lip like a layer of snow.

'Well, she handily gave a roomful of people all the information they need to poison someone, fatally or otherwise, opening up the list of suspects. She can come and go around the chapel and house as she helps with the flower arranging, which means she's well known and trusted. No one's going to think it's unusual if she's wandering around staff-only areas. She has a strong reason to want to make Kenneth suffer, and if others become ill in the process, well that only helps confuse things as we're unsure who the intended target was.'

'What's this about a list of suspects?' I hadn't seen Detective Sergeant Colette Harnby walk in. 'I assume you're talking about the skeleton in the pub and not the recent poisoning. I can cope with you doing some research around a murder that's over 100 years old. A recent case, not so much.'

'Can I get you a drink?' I asked, trying to distract her.

'Sure.'

I managed to catch Chelsea's eye. 'Black, right?'

'That's the one.' She pulled her purse out of her bag.

'No, it's on me,' I told her. 'Fancy a stollen?'

'I do, but I'm paying.'

'Come on, it's fine.'

'No, it's not.' She looked at me sternly. 'Think about it: coffee leads to cake, leads to lunch, and before you know it the police are being accused of accepting bribes. That's how it can start. I can't risk the smallest slip-up. Apart from the challenge of being a woman in this job... well, you know the rest.'

She clearly didn't want to say anything in front of Craig, but she'd recently revealed to me that she was related to her boss; Detective Inspector Mike Flynn was her uncle, and they'd agreed to keep it quiet so there wouldn't be accusations of nepotism. Craig politely pretended he was interested in some of the books on the shelves that were lining the walls. It was time to distract her again; I'd hit a nerve and knew she was right.

I tried not to think of all the coffee and cake I had given Joe. He would never move it on from there; he was the least corrupt person I knew. I'd seen less of him the last couple of weeks and put it down to workload, but maybe he was also trying to be considerate and not make things awkward now he was dating Ellie. I felt a very slight pang; I missed him, there no denying it.

'...so we seem to be coming to a grinding halt.'

I hadn't noticed that Harnby had been talking.

'Sorry, a halt?'

'Yes, the poisoning. Do you need more coffee? I have to confess, we're not getting very far. The berries are just too easy to get hold of, too many people have access to the vestry and there are so many Christmas events taking place here that CCTV simply captured the fact that there were hundreds of people on site that night.'

'Are you giving up?' I asked, surprised.

'No, we don't just give up.' She looked at Craig and smiled reassuringly. 'Apart from anything, I'd like to get a few things – this included – wrapped up before Christmas, if you'll excuse the pun.'

When I'd first met Harnby, she'd assessed me with eyes that I knew picked up on everything and I was certain she hadn't initially been very impressed. I was a nosy inconvenience who was making her department look bad. She'd been a hard nut to crack, but I think over time she had realised that I wasn't going to go away, and having me at Charleton House and the knowledge that came with that could be useful.

'What about Sian and Verity?' I asked, wondering if I could get her to slip up.

'What about them? Yes, we've interviewed them, and no, I'm not telling you what was said.'

No, no slipping up there.

'Nice try,' said Craig with amusement.

'Have you been able to give any time over to Dwin Lee?' It seemed like a safer topic that she was happier talking about.

'We have, we found a very distant relative.'

'You did what?' I nearly knocked over the mug of coffee that Chelsea had just put on the table.

'Don't get too excited. They are very distant and only had a vague idea of a relative who had gone missing in the past. There really was nothing they could tell us. They couldn't even find a photograph of him.'

I immediately felt as though all the air had been let out of me.

'But, their DNA sample has helped us be 99% certain that the body is that of Edwin Lee.'

That pepped me up again.

'Other than that, I'm betting you and Mark have more than us.'

It was true, we did, but I wasn't ready to say anything about the possible connection between the Duke's ancestor and what I was sure was a defenceless old man. I wanted to be absolutely certain, or as certain as I could be, before I started muddying those waters.

'Are you free?' Mark had called my office just as I had finished closing up the café.

'I'm free on a Friday night, let alone a Monday night. My diary is hardly jumping to the sound of parties at the best of times,' I moaned, although I was rather fond of my quiet life.

'Can you hear that? I think it might be the sound of a tiny, tiny violin. I've had a call from Steve, he's wondering if we can go round to the pub. Apparently Rosemary has found a few things that might be of interest, and I also dug up a few things at Manchester Library.'

'Really? You actually did some work? Are you sure you're not just looking for an excuse to show me what bargains you bought today? How many pairs of shoes did you buy?'

There was silence at the end.

'Come on.'

'One… or two, and then there was this other pair that…'

'So you bought three pairs of shoes. Did you buy anything for Bill?'

'Of course, what do you take me for? I found a beautiful hand-kerchief that will go perfectly with his favourite tie.'

'A hankie? You bought your long-suffering husband a hankie?'

'It's finest silk… I'm kidding, two pairs of shoes are for Bill. What kind of miser do you think I am? Are you coming to the pub or not?'

'I'll see you there, Scrooge.'

CHAPTER 20

I decided I might as well have my dinner at the Black Swan. It had been a long day and I really didn't fancy cooking.

'Fish and chips?' Steve asked. I just grinned and he made his way into the kitchen to place my order before returning to his seat. Mark, Steve and Rosemary were sitting around a table close to the fire. The crackle and pop of the burning logs could be heard over the chatter of the small Monday night crowd.

Rosemary explained the presence of the cardboard box in front of her. 'When we took over the pub, there was all sorts of rubbish up in the attic. Every previous owner must have just shoved stuff up there when they moved on and no one had bothered to go through it. I finally had a sort out last year and it's much more organised.

'There's still quite a lot of work to be done, but I tried to narrow it down to things that might be important or genuinely interesting. I roughly dated it at the time, but it still took me all afternoon to dig this out. There's not much of it because it's the oldest, and I suppose people like William Austin wouldn't have given much thought to preserving things for the future. Unlike now. We're all convinced something will be worth some money down the line, or we want to appear on some antiques TV show with our grandmother's lamp. This is stuff that either related directly to William, or from around that time.'

She slowly lifted the lid off the cardboard filing box and we all leaned forward to peer in, as though we were being granted access to the Holy Grail. I half expected a column of light to shoot up from the box into the air; I just hoped our faces wouldn't melt in the process.

I tried to hide my disappointment. Rosemary was right, there wasn't much. Various scraps of paper, a couple of bills, a pipe, some old photos.

'This was William Austin, and I guess that was his daughter, Catherine.'

I nearly snatched the photo out of her hand. Catherine was a slim girl with long hair, a nervous smile and delicate features. She wore a smart long skirt, but it looked worn along the hem, and the stains I thought I could see along the edges of the apron were probably permanent, despite hundreds of washes. Her shirt was nicely pressed and I thought I could just make out some very fine stripes. Despite the clothes looking tired, they were probably some of her best, chosen especially for the photo.

She looked weary and there were shadows under her eyes, but there was no doubt that she was pretty. I imagined her being a great draw to the pub and popular with all the working men who came in after a long day. It was also obvious why someone like George would be attracted to her. She would have caught his eye the minute he walked in the pub. Maybe he had seen her outside working and it was Catherine who had made him venture into the pub in the first place. If we were wrong and he hadn't been the kind of man who would lower himself to drinking with the estate workers, then Catherine may have been motivation enough for him to change his mind.

I looked at her father. One foot was resting on the end of a wooden bench. His chest was puffed out and he looked particularly satisfied with life, but he didn't smile. I wasn't sure many people smiled for the camera in those days, but he didn't even look like a cheerful man who was just being serious for the moment. He looked like a miserable old coot.

As hard as it is to be sure with a black-and-white photo, I guessed his shirt had started off white and gone grey over time. A pipe was poking out of the shirt pocket. Other men – customers, I assumed – stood in the background, staring at the camera with blank expressions, a mug of beer in one hand, many with a clay pipe in the other.

I looked at a second smaller picture. This time it was William alone. He looked just the same, but was smarter. He had on a black waistcoat; it was still quite worn, but he'd been without this additional layer of respectable clothing in the first photograph. A watch chain hung in a loop from button to pocket. There was no sign of Catherine. I wondered if this had been taken after his daughter had passed away; he seemed to be doing better financially, if his appearance was anything to go by.

Rosemary set a china beer mug on the table. It was fully intact and matched the fragment of one that had been found with Dwin; the markings were exactly the same.

Mark grinned at me with a satisfied expression. 'Seems my love of beer was helpful, and accurate.'

I looked through a number of invoices for a company called Millstone Brewing. A small sketch of a Derbyshire millstone was in the centre at the top of the paper. Beautiful cursive handwriting flowed across the page as if it was a love letter, not a demand for payment.

Steve took one from me and peered at it.

'Where are your glasses?' Rosemary asked.

'No idea,' was the mumbled response. She tutted and rolled her eyes at me.

'They shut down a long time ago, but for a while, Millstone

were the major brewers around here. They must have been quite a small business at this point. This one hasn't been paid,' Steve said, taking the others from me and laying them side by side. 'There are gaps – these are for February, April, October and November. February and April have been paid – see, they've been stamped and signed, but by the looks of things, they were paid quite late. He must have been stringing them along until he could get the money together each month. The October and November ones are unpaid. The brewery would have been chasing him for his money, especially if he wanted to place an order for December.'

'Is there any way of knowing if he ever paid them, or if he paid them but they weren't stamped?'

Steve shook his head. 'I doubt it.'

Mark reached across for one and joined in. 'It fits, though. Catherine mentioned her father's debts to Mary, and that her admirer had offered to help pay them off. I wonder if these are the debts she was talking about. Paying for your beer is pretty fundamental to running a pub. If he was at risk of losing the business, then she would have wanted to help her father. This looks like it's related.'

Mark was holding a yellowing piece of paper and I watched his eyes scan across the page.

'It's a letter. It's not addressed to anyone; my guess is William was putting together a letter to the brewery. If he wasn't used to writing regularly, he'd probably have tried out a number of versions before making a fair copy to send. I would guess this was one of his practice runs.'

Mark read the partial letter out to us.

"*I have grate reluctance in trubling you and a grate anxiety to please you. The monies past due to you will not be delayed much further. I have a new oportunity and future good fortunes have been promised to me, which will present to me enough money to repay that owed to yourselves.*'"

The writing was surprisingly neat, but if he was practising, then he would have been taking a lot of care over it.

'Do you think this was relating to the invoices for the brewery?' I asked.

'Not impossible, but from what we know of the man, he owed quite a lot of money, so this could have been for any of his creditors.'

'I hope some of this is helpful, there doesn't seem to be a lot.' Rosemary sighed as she put the lid back on the box.

'Are you kidding?' I exclaimed. 'We have a photo of William and Catherine, that's fantastic. It makes it so much more real, personal. That young woman's life was cut far too short, and while she was alive, it seems there was a man who made such an impression on her, she named her son after him. She must have cared for Dwin Lee a great deal. I bet she was devastated when he went missing. Now we can see the face of someone who would, I'm sure, have wanted his killer brought to justice. We can't quite do that, but we can try and solve the mystery.'

'I'll have another look. If I find anything else, I'll let you know.'

Rosemary stood, and then stepped out of the way so a young server could put my fish and chips on the table. Mark looked at my dinner.

'Hungry, much?'

'Hey, it's Christmas. I can eat what I want, it's the rules.' He stole a chip off my plate and I pretended to stab the back of his hand with a fork. Steve shook his head.

'I'll leave you kids to it. Mark, can I get you anything to eat?'

'A big bowl of chips,' I answered for him.

'Righto, they're on the way, and thanks.'

'What for?' I asked.

'Looking into this for us. It doesn't feel right knowing an unsolved murder happened here. I've felt kind of uneasy ever since we found him. As the landlord, I feel responsible in some way, like he's one of my customers, and I want to help.'

He didn't wait for either of us to respond, walking back to the bar, his broad shoulders slightly stooped. I wasn't used to seeing the endlessly cheerful publican looking down. I watched and, as he stood behind the bar, I thought I saw him take a deep breath. Then he turned to face his customers with his usual welcoming grin.

'What can I get you fellas?' he asked of two men. I knew exactly what he was doing: that was life when you worked with the public. No matter what was going on in your own life, you had to shake it off and treat each and every person who came to you like royalty, like their presence was the highlight of your day. Steve had it down to a fine art.

Once the bowl of chips had arrived and Mark had devoured every last one, including the little crispy bits in the bottom, which I consider to be the best bits, I turned the conversation to the remainder of his trip to Manchester.

'Ah yes. Ye of little faith, assuming I just spent the day bunking off. Not so.' He dug around in his rucksack and pulled out a bundle of photocopies. 'I was wondering how much more I could find out about William, especially after both Dwin and Catherine died. I figured that there might be something in the following months that was useful. Poor old William didn't have a good time of it.'

Mark laid out some of the papers. They were photocopies of old newspaper reports.

'In days of yore, everything went in the newspapers, including daily business in the courts and all sort of business news. Now, look at this.' He had highlighted a short section. 'It's from 1887.'

'*The magistrates refused to renew the licences for The Plough. Police Superintendent Wickman told the magistrates that the publican, Mr*

William Austin, had to be summoned for encouraging gambling for drink.'

'So two years after he loses his daughter, he loses his pub?'

'Pretty much. The story continues in the property section.'

'To Brewers, Publicans and others: Valuable Freehold Public House and Property, The Plough, at Hadbury to be sold by Auction on Thursday 22nd September 1887 at 5 o'clock in the evening, precisely subject to the general conditions of the sale of the Derbyshire Incorporated Law Society.'

'It must have been at this point that the Fitzwilliam-Scotts bought the pub and the land around it. I knew they'd extended the estate in that corner around this time, but I didn't know when.'

'So the Duke is effectively Steve's boss?'

'Yes, although it's part of the business side of the Charleton House Trust and the Duke won't have anything to do with the day-to-day running of the pub. But if you remember, the Duchess was involved in the redesign of the guest rooms.'

'So William never got the licence back. I guess if he was allowing gambling and taking that level of risk, he never fully sorted his debts out. Which would mean that whatever Catherine's admirer promised was never fulfilled. If whoever it was, was a genuinely nice guy with plenty of money, then you'd assume that he'd want to help William out, even though the marriage couldn't go ahead.'

'Perhaps, and George doesn't seem like the most charitable of people. But there's more, which makes it very clear that William never got any of his debts sorted, and in fact, things got worse. William loses his licence, and he's then arrested. The whole sorry state of affairs means he loses everything. He has no way to try and restore his good name, he can't continue in business, he ends up in prison!'

'Why? His debts?'

'His attempt to resolve his debts. It's here, look.' He pointed at another paragraph he had highlighted.

'*Chesterfield County Courts. Mr D A Peters, solicitor, Sheffield, has prepared a petition for adjudication in bankruptcy against William Austin, late publican, Derbyshire, and who was sentenced on Wednesday December 14th 1887 to two years' penal servitude for forgery and fraud.*'

With this, Mark had stunned me into silence. The extent of the forgery and fraud must have been pretty bad if William had been given a prison sentence. He must have been a desperate man, and desperate men do stupid things.

'Do you know what happened after that?' I asked Mark. He shook his head.

'I can't find anything else, and we know he wasn't buried with his daughter.'

'I wonder what happened to his wife, although I'm not entirely sure I want to know. I don't think I could handle any more sad stories coming out of this family.'

CHAPTER 21

A little while later, Mark and I were sharing a sticky toffee pudding. It was the perfect winter dessert. The pudding itself was light, but the flavour heavy and warming. The rich toffee sauce mixed with the enormous dollop of ice cream as it melted. We'd asked for one to share and two spoons, but Rosemary had brought out two servings in one bowl with a cheeky grin. I was going to spend the whole of the next year on a diet at this rate.

'The padre tells me the police are no closer to figuring out who the killer cook is?' Mark mumbled through an enormous mouthful of pudding.

'Killer? No one died.'

'I know, but I couldn't think of anything better.' He thought for a moment. 'The Brutal Berry Baker. Hey, that's not half bad.' He rewarded himself with an even bigger spoonful of pudding.

'No, they're not, nor am I. All four of the people round that table had irritated others, or in some cases done a lot more than irritate them. Kenneth's departure from his company really messed things up for his business partner, Esther Marsh's husband. It's impacted on her life, too; she's had to come out of retirement. She has immediate access to the berries, and the vestry. Plus she'd recently run a workshop, giving a roomful of people the knowledge needed to poison someone, which immediately dilutes the field of suspects.

'Both Sian and Verity seem to have an axe to grind against each other. Countless people are tired of Harriet, although that's not a particularly strong argument. At worse, I think that whoever did it wasn't worried about Harriet getting sick as a by-product of their actions when they knew she'd recover. Harriet herself, not a chance. She's really growing on me. She might nag you into an early grave, but she wouldn't try and speed up the process with poison.'

'So that only widens the field to what? About fifty active chapel volunteers?'

'I doubt it's that many. In all the time I've been spending round there since it happened, there's probably ten, maybe fifteen faces that I've seen regularly. A lot more will attend parties and workshops, but it's a smaller number that really get stuck into the running of things.'

'Still, that's a lot of people to work through.'

I leant back in my chair, feeling slightly defeated by it all. If there was one mystery I didn't want to fail to crack, it was this one. Craig was a good friend, and it was an awful thing to have happen within any community, but this was a small community within the boundary of Charleton House, and as a result it was important to me. It should be so simple, yet it was anything but. I kept coming back to Esther. She was the most obvious suspect and was in the best position to manipulate the whole thing, but it didn't sit quite right with me.

'You know what will help?' Mark asked.

'What?'

'A gin and tonic. Let's grease those cogs.'

. . .

We were gathering our coats and bags, and were about to roll out of the pub – we'd both undone the top button on our trousers – when my phone beeped. It was Craig.

'*Should I collect the biscuits from you in the morning or will you bring them to the chapel?*'

'Dammit!' I exclaimed. I must have sounded particularly distraught as Mark put his hand on my arm.

'What, are you okay? Did you hurt yourself?'

'No, I promised to make Craig those gingerbread biscuits that are to be given as gifts at an event he's hosting. I completely forgot.'

'Again! Someone's in trouble,' he said in a sing-song voice as a smile formed on his face.

'It's not funny. I have to make 120 gingerbread biscuits and decorate them, tonight.'

'Blimey, you're going to have a late night.'

He started towards his car.

'No you don't, Mark Boxer. Don't forget it's the season of goodwill.'

He sighed and slumped his shoulders, dropping his head to his chest.

'Alright, alright. I'll give Bill a call, see if he'll join us.'

'Tell him to bring a bottle of wine. I don't have any in and we're going to need help of the liquid kind to get through this.'

By the time Bill arrived, the first batch of biscuits were in the oven and I was cutting out Father Christmases, toy soldiers, stars, Christmas trees and various other suitable shapes for the next tray. The aroma of ginger, cloves and cinnamon was beginning to intensify.

Bill shook his head at me as he walked into the kitchen and took his coat off.

'Someone owes us big time. Luckily for you, I'd just finished marking schoolwork for the night.' Bill fitted perfectly the picture of a teacher who works crazy hours and goes above and beyond for his students.

'We can't do anything without a glass of wine in our hands,' declared Mark as he uncorked the bottle. I decided that festive pop music was going to get us through this and cranked up the volume, then I showed Mark and Bill the selection of biscuit cutters and cracked on with the next batch.

When a tray of biscuits came out of the oven, we put them outside so they'd cool down quickly and we could ice them. Luckily, it was both freezing cold and dry outside. I knew this recipe like the back of my hand; I couldn't remember a Christmas when I hadn't used it since I was about ten years old. It made the perfect gingerbread biscuits with the perfect amount of crunch on the outside and a little bit of softness in the middle. The balance of flavours was just right and almost everyone who tried them wanted the recipe. The secret was to use Dutched cocoa rather than regular cocoa powder. I was surprised how many people hadn't heard of it, but it was easy to get hold of.

It wasn't long before we had a production line going. I would mix while Bill and Mark cut the biscuits out, in between grabbing a wooden spoon and singing along to the music or doing an impromptu dance routine in the middle of the kitchen. Pumpkin had wisely decided to steer clear. I'd spotted her watching us from the kitchen door with a look of disdain on her face; I guessed we'd woken her. Without drawing attention to myself to avoid a complaint from Mark, who firmly believed I spoilt Pumpkin, I took her some treats in a saucer and put them in front of the fire. It was by way of an apology.

In what felt like no time at all, we had a good number of cold biscuits and were ready to start icing. It was simple enough; I only used white icing to pipe in the details and added colour with little round chocolate sweets in multicoloured sugar shells. They looked fantastic as the baubles on a tree, or eyes on Santa.

'So are you going to reply to Adam?'

The question took me by surprise. Mark was sitting on a counter top, taking a break while Bill and I were leaning over a rack of biscuits, both of us intermittently moaning about how much our backs were starting to ache. As I spun round, I knocked a biscuit onto the floor. It landed icing side down.

Mark was holding the Christmas card that was still on the counter with the pile of mail. 'Are you back in touch with him?' He looked confused and curious; I wasn't used to seeing uncertainty on his face.

'Are you reading her mail? Mark, put it down and mind your own business. Sorry, Soph.'

'It's okay. I'm sure I'd have told you at some point.'

'I hope so,' said Mark firmly. 'So, go on, are you back in touch with him?'

'No, no, I'm not. That came out of the blue and I was deciding what to do.'

Mark folded his arms. 'And what are you going to do?' It was very clear he had already decided what my course of action should be.

'I'm not replying,' I said.

'Really? You don't sound too convinced.'

'You can't blame her for being curious.' Bill was always the voice of reason.

'You can if the man concerned is a criminal who slept with someone else while engaged to be married, to *you*.' Mark looked at me and shrugged. 'You don't disagree, do you?'

'I guess not. It just took me by surprise, I didn't really know how I felt for the first few days after I received it. But no.'

'Days?' Mark exclaimed loudly. 'You've had this for days and you never told me?'

'Oh, shut up, Mark.' Bill pulled his husband off the counter and handed him an icing bag. 'Get piping and mind your own business.'

'Huh,' was Mark's simple response. We descended into silence as we all concentrated on the decorations and put our artistic skills to use.

'Done my lot!' Mark declared a short while later. 'Are there more?'

'Only a couple of lobsters, do you want to get them from outside?'

He mouthed *'What?'* at me.

'Lobsters. Thought it would add a bit of variety.'

As he stepped out into the cold to fetch the final tray of biscuits, Bill glanced across at Mark's artistic creation.

'Oh, for heaven's sake. Sophie, I'm sorry.' I looked at the biscuits that had caught his attention and we both turned to face Mark as he walked back in.

'Mark,' Bill said like an angry parent who was trying to keep his cool, 'put some trousers on Father Christmas. He has to work with children.'

CHAPTER 22

Despite not getting to bed until 2am, I made it into my office before any of my team, which was unusual at the best of times. I dropped the gingerbread cookies off at the vestry first, and then went to start my day.

I hung my coat on the back of my office door, pulled the bag of my favourite coffee beans out of my drawer and started the process of making my second cup of the day. I'd tried some of the Christmas themed coffees that always came out at this time of year. Despite my love of food and always being ready to try new flavours, I had yet to find a flavoured coffee that I liked. It didn't matter whether it was cinnamon or nutmeg, or any other flavour that I generally love, in coffee it just didn't seem right.

I was thinking about this as I sat down, mug of steaming coffee in hand, so it took me a moment to realise that there was a slightly unusual object on my desk. The beautifully wrapped red box had a gold ribbon and bow around it. It was Christmas so that wasn't entirely unusual in itself, and I'd already received a mountain of gifts from suppliers, but they were, almost without exception, bottles of wine or boxes of chocolates with a hastily added bow and no attempt to conceal the contents.

I gently untied the bow on the box, reluctant to spoil the lovely job that someone had made of it, and removed the lid. Inside, dark green tissue paper hid the treat that lay below it.

'Ha! Perfect!' I exclaimed as I pulled out four large, delicious-looking cookies. It was barely 8am so definitely not snack time, but that had never stopped me before.

I was about to take as big a bite as I could when I looked a little closer. Was that a chocolate chip? No, it looked like a cranberry, a perfectly festive snack. I hesitated, and then quickly put the cookie back in the box as though it might bite me. They weren't cranberries; I'd put my money on them being winterberries, and I really didn't fancy experiencing first-hand the after-effects of this seemingly innocent red berry.

I dialled DS Harnby's number. Despite the circumstances, I still felt silly calling the police to tell them some cookies had been left in the office of a café. And I didn't get quite the sympathetic response I had expected.

'I wondered how long it would take for you to annoy someone enough for them to try and poison you, Sophie. I thought about it myself in the beginning.'

My response was a coffee-infused splutter and a promise not to touch the box again. Harnby's humour was getting a little too similar to Mark's and I wasn't sure how I felt about that. I had enough smart alecks in my life.

'I must be closer than I realised.'

Joyce was sitting across from me, Harnby next to her. They both stared at me intently.

'Who have you told about your investigation? Who might know what direction it's heading in?' asked Harnby.

'No one. Well, I've run some ideas past Mark and Craig, asked questions of a couple of others, but they've only been clarifying questions. I've not pointed my finger at anyone in particular.'

Harnby sighed. 'That can be enough. Simply asking a question – no matter how innocent – can scare someone if they have reason to be worried. This is one of the endless list of reasons why I tell you not to get involved. Apart from anything else, you put yourself at risk.'

'There you go, Sophie, just think back to all the people you've spoken to about this and you can guarantee the culprit is in amongst them.' The look of satisfaction on Joyce's face would make you think we'd identified them there and then.

Harnby stood up.

'I need to get back to the station. But call me if you think of anything useful, something with hard evidence behind it.' She glanced at Joyce. 'Not gossip or conjecture.'

Craig sidled past her in the doorway and I watched as they exchanged words.

'He's not a bad-looking man. Needs to cut down on the beer, perhaps drop a trouser size.'

I turned and stared at Joyce. 'That's a bit harsh.'

'Not at all, I'm thinking about his health. I said he was good-looking.'

'You said he wasn't bad looking, that's not quite the same strength of compliment.'

'Okay, he is definitely a good-looking man, he just needs a woman to whip him into shape.'

I'd never heard Joyce talk about Craig in this way before; I was rather taken aback.

'Do you...'

'Fancy him? Give it a rest, girl. I'm old enough to be his mother and he's definitely not my type; I'm just saying...'

'Morning, ladies.'

'Morning, Father.' Joyce immediately softened her tone.

'Can I join you?' he asked

'Of course.' Joyce swept her hand out in front of her as she indicated a chair. Craig pulled his head back as she did so and I laughed.

'What?' She looked confused.

'Those bloody nails, you could have decapitated him with them. They're lethal.'

'They're a work of art. Have you seen them? Look.'

She shoved her hand under my nose. Each nail had a different reindeer on it, one of them with a red nose. Joyce's nails were generally a source of amusement to me, but this time I was genuinely impressed. They were almost up there with grains of rice that had entire landscapes painted on them.

'They're not stickers, either; each is hand-painted.'

I left Craig admiring the artwork, or doing a really good impression of someone who was interested – I wasn't sure which – and went to fetch him a coffee.

As I went behind the counter and started to make Craig's drink, I didn't pay much attention as Chelsea served a customer, but when they said thank you, I knew who it was. I turned round and watched Sian walk out, waving to Craig as she passed him.

'It's so funny seeing her out of school,' Chelsea said. 'When you're young, you can't imagine your teachers having first names, let alone full lives.'

'She was your teacher?' I asked, surprised. 'It is a small world.'

'Yes, maths. She's changed a lot from when she taught me, though; I was only about twelve. We used to call her Fat Feathers. We were quite cruel, and none of us could say her surname when we first saw it written down, so we just called her Feathers and it stuck. She's lost weight since then.'

'What do you mean, you couldn't say her surname?' I asked. 'It's Feathers, easy enough – you've just said it.'

'No, it's not, it's Featherstonehaugh. We used to say it Feather-stone-haw, how it's written, or different variations of that, trying to get it right, but of course, you say it "Fan-shaw". We would give up and just call her Feathers.'

Craig looked blank when I told him about Sian's name.

'We've always called her Feathers. That's what she told us her name was, and we'd have no reason to question it. I wonder if anyone else knows. I could ask Kenneth, he's coming in later.'

'Don't,' I said quickly. 'Don't say anything, not yet. If she's hiding something, then I don't want her to know we're onto her, give her time to make up a story. I want to see her reaction for myself.'

Finally, the cracks were beginning to show. There really was more than met the eye to the seemingly upstanding members of the community.

As I finished off for the day, there was a knock on my office door and a familiar face peered round. It was Joe.

'I was on my way home. Thought I'd see how you were doing?'

'Hey, stranger, come in. Well, you can try.'

Joe squeezed in and pushed my chair as far back into the corner as he could. He sat on my desk. I hadn't had seen him properly for weeks, if you discounted the other day in the pub when we were discussing the skeletal remains of Dwin Lee. His suit was creased, he'd removed his tie and undone the top button on his shirt. He looked as if he'd spent the day running his fingers through his hair and now it was full of static.

'I heard about the cookies this morning, are you okay?'

'I'm fine. I lost my appetite for anything sweet for the rest of the day, but I seriously doubt that will last. Do you have any idea who I should be keeping an eye on? Making sure I don't get left in a room alone with? I know you're not meant to tell me stuff, but if it keeps me safe...'

For a brief moment he looked convinced, but then it dawned on him.

'Very good, you nearly had me. You're more than capable of

taking care of yourself, you just want me to tell you what we know. Ain't happening.' He folded his arms dramatically and kept his lips tight shut.

'It was worth a try. Isn't there anything you can tell me? Not even if you're close to figuring out who did it?'

'Persistent, aren't you? No, we don't know who did it, and I don't think we're close. A couple of those who were apparently targeted, or at least were collateral damage, so to speak, they're quite interesting. They're hardly angels, but we can't tie any of them to the berries and the intention to make someone sick. Nothing that would stand up in a court of law.'

'Ah, but there is suspicion and intrigue?'

'This isn't *Midsomer Murders*. I'm not saying any more.'

'You used to be more forthcoming, before you…'

'Before I what?'

I was going to say 'started to date Ellie', but I realised that I was risking digging a very large hole if I continued in that direction.

'Before you were managed by DS Harnby.'

'Well, she's rightly a stickler for the rules. I'm learning a lot from her. She's a bit intense and she really needs to get a hobby, or a man, but she knows what she's doing.'

I liked to hear that. I wished that Harnby would give me a little more information, but I liked that she had such high standards. It meant I knew I could trust her if I needed to.

'Okay. So long as you're okay. I should go, I'm meeting E… I'm going for a drink.'

'It's fine, you can say her name, it's not a problem.'

'Yeah, I just… well, you know.'

'I think she's lovely, I'm really pleased for you. Just do me a favour.'

He looked deadly serious. 'Of course, what is it?'

'Run a comb through your hair, you look like a loo brush. That's no way to impress your new girlfriend.'

CHAPTER 23

There was no escaping the fact that the chapel was creepy at 6am. Without the noise of visitors, not even their footsteps and chatter outside the doors; without daylight streaming in through the stained-glass window, or the sound of Craig's laughter from the vestry, it was eerily quiet.

Mark and I had taken up our spot in a pew at the rear of the chapel. We'd pinned back the vestry door so that anyone who entered through the back door would be visible. They, on the other hand, wouldn't see us, sitting in the gloom of the chapel, all the lights off. If we'd set up camp in the vestry, we could have been seen through the big window that looked out onto the back lane. Craig had yet to have curtains put up.

I had decided that the only way to work out who was leaving the gifts was to catch them at it, and the gifts were always there when Craig started in the morning. That could also mean they were left the night before, but certainly today there was nothing on the desk when we had first checked before settling in on a hard wooden pew, my bottom telling me I should have brought a cushion.

'Hang on.' Mark walked down the central aisle, turning his

head to look down each pew. 'Here you are.' He disappeared briefly, then stood back up with a kneeling cushion. 'Sit on that.'

We made ourselves comfortable. I had a thermos of coffee – bugger the rules about drinking in the chapel. I'm sure I'd receive special dispensation under the circumstances.

'Did you go to church as a kid?' Mark whispered, clearly looking to fill the time. I shook my head.

'I didn't go to a church school, and my parents never took us. When I was at primary school we all traipsed along the road in pairs, holding hands, to the nearest church, but that was only for Easter and Christmas. When I joined the Brownies and then the Guides, there were a couple more occasions, but that was it.'

'I know you don't believe.' He was right. My parents had taken the approach that I should be allowed to make up my own mind, and I'd seen nothing in the world that told me there was anyone or anything with a grand plan. There was plenty I appreciated and respected about the church: the sense of community; the amazing architecture, but as soon as there was any sense of exclusion for those considered 'other', that appreciation went right out of the window. Here, though, Craig had created a welcoming community; I couldn't imagine anyone feeling they didn't belong.

'You have your own religion.' He grinned and nodded at my thermos. Ah yes, the glorious bean that I couldn't live without.

'I'm not sure if it's a religion or just a rather ferocious addiction.'

'What's the difference?' he asked with amusement.

I froze as I heard a clatter.

'Shhhh, what's that?' I whispered. It had come from beyond the main door so could have been anyone or anything, but it wasn't in the chapel and silence quickly descended again.

I sighed. Mark had a sly smile on the corner of his lips.

'You're jumpy.'

'Aren't you? This place feels different at this time of day.'

A movement caught my eye and I spun my head towards the altar.

'What was that?' I hissed. Mark leant out of the pew. I leant with him, resting my body weight on his shoulder. I hoped he wouldn't fall out, or I'd go crashing to the ground with him.

'A mouse, there's two of them. Getting in a quick morning prayer.'

I sat up and hit him. I was on edge, I couldn't deny it, and I was getting more on edge with every passing minute. I had no problem being on my own in one of the rooms of the house; I'd even sat on the stairs of the Gilded Hall with most of the lights off, hoping I would see a ghost, but this was different. Why being in a chapel made a difference, I wasn't sure. Perhaps it was the knowledge that there was meant to be a heart buried under the altar; perhaps it was all the funerals that had taken place here, or the endless shadowy corners and faces that watched over us: the carved angels above and the figures in the stained-glass windows.

I turned to look up at the private pew on the first floor where the Fitzwilliam-Scott family traditionally sat for services. I could have sworn someone was watching us. But it was empty and my imagination was getting the better of me. I took a deep breath and stared into my plastic cup of coffee. Luckily there was only half an inch in the bottom when my hand jolted and the coffee flew into the air.

'What the hell...' cried Mark.

We both turned at the sound of a door slamming and heavy footsteps. I got a quick glimpse of a figure as I tried to wipe the spilt coffee off Mark's trousers and shoes.

'Give over, it's fine, there wasn't much. Come on.'

We dashed across the chapel. In the shadows, I ran into the corner of a pew and yelped. That was going to leave a nasty bruise on my thigh. I staggered after Mark, through the door, past the dining table and into Craig's office where the figure had turned on the light.

'In the name of all that is holy!' exclaimed Peggy. 'You nearly gave me a heart attack. What are you doing?' She looked genuinely surprised. She sat down in a chair and put her hand, which was still clutching a duster, to her chest. There was a canister of spray polish in her other hand.

'Don't *do* that, I'm not a young woman.'

I looked at the desk; there was a small silver box with a red ribbon tied around it.

'Looks like he's still gettin' them,' Peggy said between deep breaths. 'They're early risers, I'll give them that, it's only... what? Twenty past six.'

I looked at Mark and he looked back at me, shrugged. Peggy had gone pale. We'd certainly surprised her, but had we surprised her leaving the box? I wasn't sure.

After she'd calmed down, Peggy had set about cleaning the office. I'd made us all coffee and she sipped hers in between dusting and hoovering. Mark and I sat at the dining table and had a whispered conversation.

'If it wasn't her, how did we miss them?'

'Because you were busy being freaked out by mice and footsteps, that's how. Anyone could have crept past while you clung on to me, I swear you've drawn blood.'

'I have not. So we got up early for nothing.'

'Not really,' he said with a positive note in his voice. 'We know they get here early, very early, which limits the number of possible suspects, and security will have a record of everyone who goes through the gates.' His voice returned to a normal level as Peggy came out of the office.

'It reduces them, that's for sure, but there's still quite a few people around from about six on. All the cleaners on early shift, deliveries, the gardeners start early. Security themselves. If the events team have got a breakfast event, then they'll be onsite at the crack of dawn, setting up. On a busy day you could still be talking a hundred or so, and almost all would have reason to come down that back lane and pass the door into the vestry.'

Peggy wandered off into the chapel. As a volunteer, she took it upon herself to do a bit of extra unofficial cleaning in the chapel. It was the main reason the place gleamed.

Mark had a serious look on his face.

'Why are you so bothered about the gifts? It's a bit creepy, but there doesn't seem to be anything malicious about it, and presumably it will stop after the 25th.'

'It was something Chelsea said, about whoever added the berries to the mulled wine being like an attention-seeking teenager. Well, I think it's exactly the same with the gifts. Whoever poisoned the wine is also leaving the gifts for Craig – even you suggested it. I still think they have a grudge against someone at that meeting, but they're also trying to get Craig's attention. Crack this and we kill two birds with one stone.'

'Or poison them with the one berry,' he suggested.

I was thinking about heading to my office and beginning my work day properly when the back door to the vestry burst open and Harriet marched in like she owned the place. She wore a long burgundy coat with the collar up high and a matching woolly hat pulled down tight over her ears. I noticed that the hat had been patched more than once in its lifetime.

'It's far too early for a meeting, so why are you all cluttering up the place?' she demanded.

'You know full well what I'm doing here,' replied Peggy firmly from the door to the chapel.

'Not you, I'm used to seeing you here, whether you're needed or not. It's these two…' She trailed off as she reached the open door into the chapel. 'Is that…? I can smell…' She pushed past

Peggy. 'Coffee! Why can I smell coffee? The rules are perfectly clear, no food or drink. What the devil?'

I closed my eyes and sighed; I'd forgotten about the coffee I'd spilt on Mark as we'd dived out of the pew. Harriet must have found the puddle of brown liquid.

'PEGGY! I need you here, NOW!'

Peggy brandished her mop like a weapon.

'Wish me luck.' She followed the sound of Harriet's voice as the elderly woman continued to complain loudly about a lack of respect and the permanent damage that could be done by the evil chemicals in coffee. I grabbed hold of Mark's arm.

'Come on, while she's distracted.' We bolted for the door like a pair of criminals fleeing the scene. I might have been developing a soft spot for Harriet, but I would forever be terrified of being on the receiving end of her wrath.

Mark went one way, towards his office, and I went to fetch my post from the mail room. We had our own onsite 'mail man', Al, who sorted through the post and then delivered it round the offices. At this time of year, he was swamped as everyone did their Christmas shopping online and had the parcels shipped to work where there was someone to sign for them twenty-four hours a day.

Al was juggling parcels and trying to find somewhere to put them on his cluttered counter tops.

'Morning, Sophie.'

'Al, don't stop. I'll just grab mine.'

'Cheers, darlin'. Oh, Soph, can you do me a favour?'

'Anything.'

'Harriet dropped an envelope on the way out earlier. Can you give it to her when you see her? I'll only get a lecture off her for taking my eye off the ball and I could do without that today.'

I smiled knowingly and picked up the letter. Considering the spilt coffee in the chapel, I decided I'd better take the safe option of handing it to Craig to deliver; I too could do without a lecture.

As I left Al to it, stepping back out, I almost slammed straight into Sian.

'Oh sorry, Sian, but wait. Can I have a word?'

She didn't look very happy. 'I'm in a rush.'

'It won't take a minute, Ms Feathers. Or is it Featherstonehaugh?'

She came to a sudden stop and stared at me. 'I have no wish to talk to you.' Then she set off again.

I stayed where I was. She was never going to talk to me in that mood.

CHAPTER 24

I knew that I would get to talk to Sian eventually. She couldn't ignore me forever, and besides which, it was the volunteers' Christmas party this evening and she was bound to be there, especially as one of the organisers. So I distracted myself with the other mystery in my life.

I couldn't believe it had taken me this long to act on the rather tantalising information that Gretchen Dangerfield had given us. I'd been longing to look more carefully at the objects Mary Ollerenshaw had stolen from George, but the job I was paid to do had been getting in the way. I wasn't complaining; I particularly loved my job at this time of year, but still, I wanted to get to the bottom of Dwin's death.

Going to the stores on a weekday was taking a risk. If I was caught, the worst I'd get was a rather severe slap on the wrist, but I didn't want to damage my reputation. I knew the conservation department had a meeting every Wednesday morning, so they wouldn't be around, and Mark had picked up the key for me when he'd first arrived on site this morning, although he couldn't join me as he was delivering back-to-back tours all day. It was the curators who might find me, but that was a chance I was just going to have to take, and I hoped that 8am was too early for them.

I ran up the stone steps and said good morning to the pigeons who were sheltering from the cold, wet day outside. At least if they were in here, they weren't finding a way into the main building and pooping on valuable tapestries or furniture, which was a real concern when a bird got in.

This time, I no longer viewed the storeroom as boring. Instead, it held endless possibilities. I scanned the shelves, wondering what fascinating stories lay between the pages of each book. Row after row after row held evidence of people and their adventures, people I had yet to meet, and I wanted to move in here with a supply of coffee, a couple of pillows and a blanket, make myself comfortable and devour their stories. But I had to be patient; there was one story I had to focus on first.

I quickly found the box containing Mary's diary and put it on the table. After carefully removing the lid, I laid it to one side and focused on the other smaller objects. The first objects weren't of any particular value, but could easily be seen as trinkets collected by a love-sick teenager: a couple of buttons, a comb, a small piece of soap. Anything that had been touched by George would no doubt have been of great value to Mary, but unlikely to get her fired.

A beautiful black and gold fountain pen, engraved with the initials GHFS, looked as good as new, and that was something I could imagine her losing her job over. Back then, pens were very much a luxury item. In a small cloth bag was a pocket watch, another valuable item. She was lucky not to have been reported to the police, assuming, of course, that she hadn't been. There was a collection of visiting cards; similar to business cards, they were a sign of social status, and were often left to indicate that someone had visited while you were out.

Some scraps of paper held what I assumed was evidence of George's handwriting: a title of a book; part of an address; a theatre ticket from London with a woman's name written on it. There was a note from what appeared to be an old school friend, saying how nice it was to run into George at a dinner party, and a letter inviting him on a shooting weekend in Scotland. Other bits and pieces would have been rubbish to most people, but for Mary, they were a connection to a man she could never have.

A small note appeared to refer to some business or other: *'I forsee no further problems, and posess no doubt that which we spoke can now progress. I know we are all of a happy mind. Perhaps you could take some time from your day and we can plan for payment and arrangements of the great event'.*

I couldn't resist getting the diary out of the box and continuing to read. Mary was catty and clearly loved gossip, and I let time slip by as I immersed myself in her daily life. Fully aware that she would eventually lose her job, I wondered where she had gone. Had she managed to get another job or did she end up destitute? It was a very quick road to poverty in those days.

I leaned in as Catherine Austin got another mention. Only Mary's comments were no longer those of a friend. As the diary went on, she was describing Catherine as two-faced, that she had stuck a dagger in Mary's heart. Mary hoped that her friend's betrayal would turn back on her and she would be left ugly and alone. As I'd read earlier about their friendship, the words seemed particularly vicious. Whatever Catherine had done, Mary was furious and had been badly hurt, and by mid-December, Catherine was public enemy number one.

Mary had not been old enough to really process what had happened, so like any teenager, she'd turned to hate and anger. The words appeared to have been spat onto the page, the writing messier, more jagged than before. I could only hope that if Mary had confronted Catherine, no matter what her former friend had done, she'd toned her anger down just a notch or two.

I made a few more notes, and then carefully packed everything away, having to hold myself back from pulling another book off the shelf or opening a few more boxes. It was a long time since I had formally studied history at university, and it was partly my fascination with the past that had brought me here to Charleton House. But I rarely had time these days to do anything other than flick through the various books that filled my bookcases at home.

I left the room, determined to find the time to get back to the subject that had fascinated me since I was at school. When I eventually moved on from Charleton, I didn't want to look back and regret that I hadn't made the most of my time here.

CHAPTER 25

I had made it back to the café to help with the lunchtime rush. In between talking to a customer who complained there was too much chocolate in their chocolate brownie and another who was furious that our tables weren't all of the exact same design and therefore looked 'scruffy', I served dozens of turkey and stuffing rolls, ending up with gravy all down my front, and quickly ran out of stollen.

I watched as Chelsea took the time to entertain a small child who wouldn't stop crying and received from the mother the most grateful, exhausted smile that I had ever seen. Almost every member of staff who came in to buy lunch told me how pleased they were that I was doing a reading at the staff Christmas service, and the nerves that bubbled up every time I heard it meant I lost my appetite.

Once the café quietened down, I sat at a small table with my notes, and before I could say, 'You deserve a pay rise', Chelsea appeared with a mug of coffee. I was reading through my notes when a shadow appeared across my notepad.

'Hello, you're the manager, right?' I looked up at a young

woman who had metal all over her face. Pierced ears, nose, a row of small rings along the line of her eyebrow.

'I am, can I help?'

'I'm looking for Chelsea.'

'I'm here, Jess.' Chelsea ran across the café, untying her apron. 'I won't be a moment.' I must have looked confused. 'I booked the afternoon off. Is that still okay? I mean, I can… well, I could do another…'

'Of course, you go. Doing anything nice?'

'Chels promised me a tour of this place, I've never been before.' There was a tapping sound as Jess talked.

'Sorry, this is Jess, my cousin. This is Sophie, my boss.'

'Nice to meet you.' I shook Jess's hand.

'Chels loves working here, she talks about it all the time.' There it was again, tap, tap, tap.

'We love having her here,' I replied. Chelsea had her coat on and her rucksack over her shoulder.

'Leave your bag with me,' I offered. 'Put it in my office, no point lugging it around.'

Chelsea smiled and disappeared for a moment before returning and looping her arm through that of her cousin.

'Now go and enjoy yourselves,' I instructed them. As Jess turned to go, I saw something glinting in her mouth. Blimey, she even had her tongue pierced. I wasn't sure if getting that done required bravery or stupidity. Whatever it was, I certainly didn't have enough of it.

Joyce passed them as they left.

'Heavens, it's a good job we don't have metal detectors in the building, she'd send them into overdrive. Why on earth do people do that? I bet she's so pretty under all that metal. Young people.' She shook her head as she sat down. 'I'm so glad I'm beyond all that experimenting.'

I looked at the lime green eye makeup and turquoise cashmere sweater she was wearing. She was still more than capable of experiments of her own, only they seemed to involve finding new ways to resemble members of the animal kingdom. Every now and again, her outfit veered towards the peacock.

'You look like Mark when he's caught up in a good book, what are you thinking about?' She craned her neck and scanned the room. 'Are you on your own? Where are your staff? I want a coffee.'

'Let me…'

'Stay where you are. You need to be more forceful with them.' She walked to the counter. 'Excuse me, excuse me.' She tapped her knuckles on it. 'I'd like a coffee and your manager is out here, timing how long it takes for someone to come and serve me.'

A young man's terrified face appeared from the kitchen. He would have recognised Joyce's voice and was now probably wishing that he could suffer a stroke on the spot and not have to serve her.

He glanced at me and I shook my head, mouthing, *I'm not.*

'Yes, she is,' Joyce said firmly. How did she know what I'd just mouthed? The woman must have an extra set of eyes on the back of her head, hiding under the back-combed hair-sprayed mountain of hair. 'I'll have a coffee and… what cake has least sugar in in?'

'Give her one of the lavender cupcakes,' I shouted across the room. 'It matches her outfit.'

The young server glanced nervously at Joyce.

'Do as she says,' Joyce demanded. 'I'll be sat over there.'

She settled back at the table next to me and I stared at her.

'What? You need to keep them on their toes.' She snapped her fingers a couple of times. 'They need to pick up the pace. So what is it? Are the clues coming together? The name of the poisoner is on the tip of your tongue, but you can't quite grab it?'

'It's not that, it's the skeleton, Dwin. I have all this information floating around and I'm trying to piece it together. If I tell you something, do you swear not to say a word, to anyone?'

She mimed zipping her lips together.

'Okay, well the evidence we have so far is starting to point towards the possibility that George Henry Fitzwilliam-Scott could have been involved in the murder. I'm not sure he killed Dwin himself, he might have paid someone. Either way, it's not something that sits comfortably with me. Can you imagine having to go and talk to the Duke and Duchess and tell them there's a murderer in the family?'

'Hmm, it's unlikely to get you a promotion.'

I told Joyce about the falling out between Catherine and Mary.

'Definitely a man,' she concluded. 'Two young women fall out, it's bound to be about a man. Catherine has already told Mary that a Prince Charming has entered her life. At that age, girls are always falling out over who they fancy, or whatever the word is. This sounds no different. *Of course* it's George that's the cause of the fight. If Mary is obsessed with him, then he's the only thing on her mind, all she ever thinks about. He's the only one who would cause that response in her, which of course proves one thing for certain.'

'What's that?' I asked.

'George is Catherine's admirer. Which would also confirm that he is the father of her child.'

'How do you know that for sure?'

'Have you come across anything that gives you the impression that Catherine is anything other than a good girl? She works hard for her father; Mary says nothing about her running around with various young men. The small amount of information you've told me says she's a well-behaved, hard-working girl, unlike Mary who is clearly wayward.

'You told me that Catherine talks about being in love, refers to a gentleman who can help her father. That seems to be important to her; she's considerate, wants to help her remaining family. She's a thoroughly good girl in my book.'

That was saying something coming from Joyce, whose morals could be described as a little loose around the edges.

'It's a shame she's fallen for such a cad, then.'

'Indeed. Although we all need a little excitement in our lives.' Joyce winked at me and placed a piece of cupcake in her mouth seductively. At least, I assumed that was what she was trying to portray.

'I doubt it's the exciting side of him that she saw if he was trying to seduce a good girl, especially if he promised to take care of her and her father.'

'You think he was just trying to get into her bed?' Joyce asked as she licked the last bit of icing off her fingers.

I nodded. 'Definitely. Look at the timeline. George spends his time trying to seduce Catherine. She resists. Let's assume Catherine is herself in a moral quandary about it, but then Dwin, who is also advising her against it, vanishes. The following year, let's say around the nine-month mark, Catherine gives birth. But that doesn't work with the idea of her being a "good girl". You'd think she'd be unlikely to sleep with someone outside of marriage, no matter what he promised her.'

'If she trusted him; if he'd reassured her that he was going to do the "right thing"; if she thought it would help her father by ensuring her marriage into a wealthy family. There are endless reasons why a good person does something outside the boundaries of respectability, all with good intentions behind them. What about Dwin, why would she listen to him in particular?'

Joyce was really talking sense, I was glad I'd confided in her.

'I believe he was more of a father to her than her true father. She even named her son after him. George viewed Dwin as a stumbling block and either he killed him, or he paid someone who worked at the house and who had a reputation for violence to kill him.'

'Do you have strong evidence of this?' Joyce looked a little concerned. 'You need to be sure.'

'No, I don't, not yet.'

'Well it's not like you to give up on anything. If the evidence is out there, you'll find it.'

Her belief in me was comforting, but I knew there was a strong chance that we might not *ever* have a solid case. We could be pretty certain of what happened, but it wouldn't be enough to succeed in a court of law, were the various people involved alive today. That was a disheartening thought, but I was determined to get as close as I possibly could.

Joyce eventually left me to it, taking a second cupcake with her and wishing me luck. I sat staring at the photos I'd taken of the objects that Mary had stolen, wondering if there was something there that would be useful. There had been something familiar about one of the items, but I couldn't be sure which one.

I'd loved having something tangible from the past in front of me, something that one – or more – of the people involved in my century-old mystery had touched. I've long felt that the events that have occurred within a building come to inhabit its fabric, almost like a shadow that lives on within the bricks. It's hard to explain, especially for someone who isn't religious and doesn't believe in the afterlife, but something must linger.

I needed more, more connections to the past. I phoned Tina, my Library Café supervisor who was currently helping out at the Stables Café, and asked if it was quiet enough for her to return here so I could leave for an hour. It was, so I grabbed my coat and bag and left as soon as she walked through the door.

I wanted to get up close to history.

CHAPTER 26

*A*s I dashed across the car park, I saw Mark. He was saying goodbye to one of his tour groups as they climbed on board a coach. I grabbed his arm.

'Are you free now?'

'For an hour, then I've another group.'

'Great, come with me.'

'But I…'

I didn't let him finish. I bundled him into the car and shot out of the car park, ignoring the 5 mph signs.

'What's the emergency?' Mark asked as he hurriedly fastened his seatbelt.

'There isn't one, but if we've only got an hour, I don't want to waste any time.'

'I haven't eaten lunch yet.'

'Perfect, we're off to the pub. You can eat there.'

The Black Swan was busy. Most of the customers would have been to Charleton House to enjoy the Christmas decorations and do some shopping before coming here for a lazy lunch and afternoon in front of the fire. I sent Mark off to a table with a menu, and then leaned over the bar and called into the kitchen.

'Rosemary… Rosemary.'

She popped her head round the door. 'Hello, Sophie, everything alright?'

'Sorry to disturb you, but could I see that box of objects again?'

'Of course, love. I'll be right with you.' She wiped her hands on her apron and made her way to a door at the far end of the bar. I returned to Mark.

'I'm assuming this is your treat,' he said. 'Seeing as you dragged me in here.'

'Yes, go on then.'

Fortunately, Rosemary offered him a sandwich on the house when she returned with the box.

'Don't think you'll get away with it that easy, Lockwood. You're buying me dinner next time. What are we doing here anyway? I didn't think there was anything useful in here.' He rooted around the box, looking at everything half-heartedly. 'What we need is evidence that ties George to Michael who worked on the estate.'

'I agree. The more I think about it, the more I believe that George wouldn't have killed Dwin himself. He wouldn't get his hands dirty.'

'Is this rush of enthusiasm something to do with your earlier visit to the stores? And please don't tell me you got caught.'

'I didn't get caught, and maybe. Something in that box was familiar and I don't know why. I just needed to see these things again. It's like a jigsaw puzzle and these are the pieces.' I brought up the photos on my phone and handed it to Mark. 'Your turn – does anything stand out?'

He sat in silence as he flicked through the images, zooming in occasionally.

'No wonder she was fired, that pen looks expensive. Mind you, she could have lost her job for taking anything, no matter how insignificant.'

I went through the box again. There it was: the letter that William had been practising. I turned the paper to show Mark just as he turned the phone in my direction. He had come to the photo of the note that declared a business deal could now move forwards, the one obstacle had been removed. It was dated 10 December, and it was in the same handwriting as the note I had in my hand.

William Austin had sent that note to George.

I found the invoices for Millstone Brewing. 'So they were working together in some way, and whatever it was could go forward.'

'Do you think this is what it's all about?' asked Mark. 'The whole Catherine thing is just a distraction? What could William and George be up to that could result in Dwin's death? Don't forget, he wasn't accidentally killed. He was clearly hit on the head. Might there have been some kind of business deal and Dwin was in the way? Did he overhear them talking about something that wasn't entirely legal? William was found guilty of forgery and fraud – maybe they were in on it together, but George was able to make sure there was no evidence of his involvement. Was Dwin involved in whatever it was?'

I wasn't convinced about his last suggestion.

'Dwin was a very poor, kindly old man. He wasn't involved in any kind of business himself. I can't imagine he had the slightest knowledge or interest in the running of the pub. He just wanted to be able to go and have a drink, when he could afford it.'

I saw Mark glance at his watch.

'Hell, I have to go, otherwise I'll have the North Yorkshire Family History Association up in arms. I'm due to start their tour in ten minutes. Come on.'

I gathered the contents of the box back together and thrust it into Rosemary's arms before we ran out of the door. Risking the wrath of my security colleagues by doubling the estate speed limit, I dropped Mark off next to the coach as it disgorged its contents, a large group of bright-eyed, excited elderly folks. I assumed that many of them had made a connection between themselves and members of the Fitzwilliam-Scott family, or perhaps some of the estate workers. I hoped for their sake that none of them were related to Michael Hall, otherwise they were likely to have a darker family history than they would perhaps hope for.

The chapel volunteers' Christmas party, like the staff party, was taking place in the Garden Café. My chef was providing a simple buffet and a number of my café assistants were working over-time, so after an hour in my office, I went over to see if they needed any help. An electrician was sitting on the floor, trying to get the lights on one of the Christmas trees to work, and a couple of cleaners were giving the inside of the floor-to-ceiling windows a wash. One of the volunteers was setting up a display of photographs that illustrated everything they had done that year. Large groups of smiling faces beamed out with various historic buildings behind them from coach trips they had been on: York Minster, Chester Cathedral, and a weekend trip to Edinburgh that I knew Peggy had organised in the early spring. Some of them had volunteered their time to clean some of the gravestones at St Anne's church and there were photos of them on their knees, hard at work.

A small selection of kneeling cushions that had been designed and stitched by a group of volunteers were proudly on display, their bright colours picking out designs from the stained-glass window that glowed over the chapel itself. Father Craig was looking at the kneelers and fussing over the proud-looking woman who was pointing out which one she had done. She looked as though the class teacher had just told her she'd received an A for her work.

Verity was helping my chef, Gregg, set up the mulled wine

table. A beautiful copper pot had been placed on a rest that was made of ornate curled pieces of cast iron. It looked rather industrial, and yet delicate at the same time. A number of small tea lights had been placed underneath, and once the hot aromatic liquid was in the pan, they would keep it warm. Rows of robust looking glass mugs were laid out; dried slices of orange, bundles of cinnamon sticks tied with red bows and little sprigs of holly were dotted about the table. The gold detail on the tablecloth was picked out by the gleaming copper pot. The overall effect was really lovely, Verity had done a good job. I just hope the mulled wine was worth it.

Verity sidled up to me. 'I assume you'll be trying some?' It sounded like a demand rather than a question. 'It's far more interesting than the stuff people normally dole out at parties, you can even buy that in bottles now. Just pour it in a pan, heat it up and you're done. Horrible. This is different. Port, that's the key.'

I smiled. 'I look forward to it.'

Verity jangled as she moved. Her wrists were full of gold bangles. She wasn't going to be sneaking up on anyone tonight. Her dark brown hair was partly secured up at the back, but she had long flowing tendrils that rested on her shoulders. Her bottle-green sweater had tiny speckles of gold woven in which glinted as she moved. She looked extremely elegant and only slightly tipped over into the 'bit much' category. It was the hair that did it; it was too perfect a uniform colour. I wondered how much grey, or even white was hidden under the dye.

Although my staff were providing sandwiches and other savoury nibbles, the volunteers had decided they wanted to provide their own cakes and Harriet was overseeing the layout of the dessert table. She had created stands of varying heights by using different-sized plastic boxes and hiding them under a red tablecloth. I assumed it was her own offering that took centre stage on the highest plinth at the back. I guessed it was a Christmas cake, the smooth white icing the backdrop for a group of choirboys in red robes made out of fondant icing, hymn books held in their perfectly formed little hands, mouths open in song. There were seven exquisite little boys and I had no doubt that Harriet had painstakingly sculpted every one: a blond lad with freckles; a brown-haired boy with lovely eyelashes. One was winking and had a cheeky grin that was so lifelike, I could have sworn that any minute, I would hear him giggle. I doubted that anyone would want to slice into it, and I imagined that was the point. It was edible, but Harriet had created a work of art and she was making sure everyone would see it as they came to choose a piece of cake.

It was interesting how she was happy to display this, but her paintings remained largely a secret. I made a note to ask her about it one day, if I ever stopped irritating her long enough to hold a proper conversation with her.

Sian and Kenneth were nowhere to be seen. Everyone looked so innocent. Fortunately, they also looked healthy and well, and no one looked as though they could coldly and calculatedly poison someone. No one ever really looked like a criminal, or at least that was what I'd decided, having met more murderers than I'd imagined possible during my time at Charleton House.

I thought again about Esther, the only one with a clear axe to grind. I was determined to keep an eye on her this evening. Who knew, maybe she'd try something else.

CHAPTER 27

*I*t was four o'clock and the house was closing. The last of the visitors were most likely in the gift shop, which remained open a little longer than the main house, hopefully spending a small fortune. I was putting chairs on the tables so I could clean the floors before returning to the volunteers' party when Chelsea came in with Jess, going to my office to retrieve her bag.

'Did you enjoy yourself?' I asked Jess.

'Yes, this place is awesome. I can't believe I've never been here before. I'm bringing my mum next time.'

We didn't have anything else to say and in the silence she tapped her tongue piercing against her teeth again until Chelsea reappeared.

'Right, I'll show Jess out then get changed. I won't be long.'

'Bye, Jess, nice to meet you.'

Jess smiled and gave a little wave. I really hoped she wasn't going to ask for a job. I'd have the awkward task of telling her she had to remove every bit of metal from her face, apart from standard earrings, before she could join us.

Mark wandered in, looking tired and very wet.

'Bloody rain. I may as well grow gills and be done with it.' He collapsed into one of the armchairs and put his feet on a coffee table in front of him. I swatted them off.

'Eh, people put their food on that.'

'Huh,' he grunted and closed his eyes for a moment before removing his tie and tossing that onto the coffee table instead.

'Long day?' I asked, knowing the answer. He loved his job, but talking non-stop all day, taking hundreds of questions, some of them utterly ridiculous, and remaining cheerful and polite throughout had clearly taken its toll. Not to mention our early start to 'attend' chapel.

'I'm guessing you don't have any alcohol in here?'

'I don't, and even if I did, you wouldn't be getting any of it. You'd have your head back, mouth open and snoring like a pneumatic drill in no time.'

'I never snore!' he exclaimed. I knew from Bill that he did, all the time.

I leant my mop against the wall, took a chair back down off a table and sat on it, placing the photo of George that I had been carrying around in my back pocket on the table in front of us.

'Remind me I need to return that to the Duke. I've been meaning to do it all day.'

'That's the other reason I'm tired,' Mark said. 'I'm trying to do my job, but with George rattling around in my brain, I forgot what I was talking about on two of the tours. Very embarrassing.'

'I'm wondering how the Duke and Duchess are going to take it if we have to tell them George was a murderer.'

'I don't think they'll be too fazed; I'm sure if you go back far enough, there's already a few in the family tree. This one, though—' he picked up the photo '—look at those cheekbones, and that moustache – it's perfect. I wish I could get mine as neat as that.'

Bill often complains about the amount of time Mark spends perfecting the various different moustache shapes and styles he's had over the years. Mark's own facial hair was perfect, too; he had nothing to be envious of.

'It's a shame he was such a rake. I completely understand why women fell under his spell. No matter what his reputation, I'm sure every woman believed him when he said he'd change, that they were the true one and he could give them a wonderful life and they'd be short of nothing. I'd believe him.'

'Shame you're not his type, and he's dead,' I said, shattering his fantasies.

'Let a man dream,' he complained. Turning the picture round in his fingers and looking at the back, he squinted and changed the position of the photo before getting up and standing under one of the sconce lights and peering even more closely. He sat back down and placed the photo on the table, looking across at me.

'Well, George Henry Fitzwilliam-Scott is not Dwin Lee's killer.'

'How do you know that?' I asked, my voice getting a bit high-pitched.

'The Duke said the photo was taken at a Christmas party, the party when George first met his future wife. It's very faint, but if you look closely there's a date on the back of that. It's the Saturday Dwin was killed. George was in London, it couldn't have been him.'

After I'd sent Mark home and smartened myself up a bit, I went back to the Garden Café where the party had finally kicked off. A group of carollers had set up near the door, each wearing a garish Christmas sweater, and they launched into a rendition of 'God Rest Ye Merry Gentlemen' as I entered. Craig was talking to the Duchess who was wearing a very warm-looking cream sweater.

She was a handsome woman, rather than pretty. Her features were strong; she looked determined and single-minded. She laughed easily and always looked comfortable at parties; she was superb at small talk. I assumed that came from a lifetime of having to attend big, fancy functions, and host many of her own.

Craig raised his glass at me, and once the Duchess had left his side to talk to Sian and admire her display, he came over and stood next to me.

'Fancy a glass of mulled wine?' he asked with a cheeky smile.

'Funnily enough, I don't. I'm sure it's fine, it's just…'

'Don't worry, I feel the same way. I can't imagine anyone trying it on here, but all the same.' He pretended to shudder. 'I'm sticking to bottled beer that I open myself. Only way to be sure.'

I watched Verity as she grabbed everyone who came within ten feet of the mulled wine and told them all about its link to Charles Dickens, noticing she would glance towards Kenneth from time to time. He'd arrived with Sian, but was now enjoying the company of a group of men who were laughing loudly as one told a story. They did look rather like a gathering of accountants on a work's night out.

'Odd lot,' observed Craig. 'A couple of awkward buggers in the mix. But they all do their bit. Many come and go, but you always get the stalwarts.'

I looked at Harriet as he said this. She was talking to the Duke about the kneelers; she must be responsible for one of them. Craig laughed as he watched Peggy grab hold of an unsuspecting man and twirl him around in time to the music that provided a backing track to the chatter and clink of glasses.

'She works so hard. She used to do a lot more with the chapel, helped organise the last Christmas party. The trip to Edinburgh was the last thing she was very involved in. I always see her working now. Maybe she needs more money, I don't know, but she certainly does more cleaning shifts than she used to. She's at every service, though, and I know she cleans the vestry more thoroughly than any other part of the house.'

Peggy straightened the gold bow in her hair and joined a small group by the window.

'Verity has offered to organise the next weekend away. It's a great relief; I just don't have the time, and without Peggy to plan it, I wasn't sure it was going to happen. We're going to have a coach trip down to Stratford-upon-Avon. I'm rather looking forward to it, I'm very keen on the Bard.'

Chelsea was collecting glasses and helping Gregg, my chef, lay out the buffet. She was wearing a Santa hat and sparkling flat red shoes – I'd told her she didn't have to adhere strictly to the dress code for this party and could add a few festive touches.

Kenneth walked over to us at the same time as Chelsea came our way.

'Where's Toto?' he asked her.

'Who?' She looked around the room.

'Toto, *The Wizard of Oz*. You're wearing Dorothy's ruby red slippers.'

'Oh these.' She looked at me. 'I hope they're okay.'

'Are you kidding? I think they're fantastic.'

She looked relieved and took the glasses she was carrying to the kitchen. Sian stopped her and added another empty glass to the tray.

'Kenneth, how much do you know about Sian? Are you good friends?'

'Yes, I'd say so.'

'Have you any idea why she doesn't use her full name while she's here?'

'What do you mean?' He looked genuinely confused. My question didn't seem to have triggered any sort of recognition.

'Sian Featherstonehaugh,' I said, spelling it out. 'Why does she go by Feathers while she's here? She used to be Chelsea's maths teacher, and Chelsea told me that her name is actually Featherstonehaugh. Have you any idea why she'd do that?' Kenneth seemed to have gone a little pale. 'Are you alright?' I asked.

'Featherstonehaugh?' he asked, using the correct pronunciation. 'Really?'

'Kenneth, are you sure you're okay?'

'Yes, yes, absolutely, it just threw me for a moment.' He blustered a little as he spoke. I wasn't in the slightest bit convinced.

'Come on, we'll go and get some fresh air.' I bundled Kenneth out of one of the patio doors before he could argue. We stood under an umbrella with a heat lamp that had been turned on for smokers who wanted to come out here and get a quick nicotine hit.

'What is it?' I asked. 'Does this have anything to do with the poisoning?'

Kenneth seemed to be staring into space so I rested my hand on his arm.

'It doesn't matter how insignificant it might seem, if it helps...'

'I know, I'm thinking. That name, the way it's written is so different from how it's pronounced. That's the kind of thing you don't forget.'

He took a deep breath out, and then perched on the edge of the heavy cast-iron table, his arms folded.

'Not long before I left the accounting firm, a complaint was made against me by a man called Featherstonehaugh. He was one of my clients. He submitted his tax returns, but ignored the advice I'd given him, was investigated and ended up with an almighty bill. He claimed I had given him bad advice and pursued me for the money. None of what he said was true.

'He complained to the Institute of Chartered Accountants, they investigated and their report came out in my favour. But it was one of the things that made me take early retirement. I was tired and I'd had enough. I only ever met this man, this Featherstonehaugh, but he was forever talking about his sister, a maths teacher, how she'd pointed out issues with my advice, said there were inaccuracies and contradictions. Of course, she was ultimately proven wrong. I never met her, but I suspected she was the driving force behind the complaint.

'When they lost and I was vindicated, she phoned and told me how hard done by her brother had been, that they would appeal and I should be prepared to lose next time. She just sounded like an interfering woman. I'd already decided to retire and set the wheels in motion to make that happen sooner than originally planned.

'I never heard from her or her brother again. I imagined he would be happy to let it all go, but his sister... well, the woman on the phone and Sian don't sound alike, not really, so I never connected them. Sian is much softer. I've never heard her get angry, but I suppose we can sound a little different on the phone, especially if we're emotional. My hearing's also not what it was.' He pointed to a tiny flesh-coloured hearing aid that I hadn't spotted before. 'I only got round to getting this after I retired.'

'How serious was the case against you?' I asked.

'Do you mean was it enough for them to want to do harm to me? That's all relative, surely. What offends one person, another can brush off. An annoyance for one can haunt another and make them want to seek revenge. Now I think about it, Sian doesn't take prisoners. She's talked about friends from the past who she's fallen out with because they made what I would view as a fairly small mistake.'

Through the window of the Garden Café, I could see that more volunteers had arrived. Everyone appeared to be having fun, except one person who was standing at the window, watching Kenneth and me. Half concealed behind a Christmas tree, Sian locked eyes with me, and then turned and disappeared.

'Kenneth, go back inside and warm up.' I dashed through the door and into the throng of people; there was no sign of Sian.

Craig appeared beside me. 'You alright? You look a bit tense.'

'Have you seen Sian?'

'She's just left.'

CHAPTER 28

I dashed out of the party and down a corridor lined with paintings of horses, some with riders astride them in hunting gear, some on their own, proud and strong with shining coats and scenes of the Charleton estate behind them. Sian had already made it down the corridor and round the corner, out of sight.

I eventually burst out into the chill evening air. A member of staff flattened themselves dramatically against the wall.

'What's on fire, Soph?' they called after me, laughing. Round another corner and I could see down the cloisters past the chapel door, but there was no sign of Sian. She couldn't be all that much faster than me, surely? I thought about the box of chocolates on my desk that I'd helped myself to every couple of minutes throughout the day, and realised it was entirely possible that even with a broken leg, she could be faster than me.

I came to a stop by the chapel door; it was ajar a couple of inches. Pushing as slowly as I could to try to avoid the creaks and groans that came from its hinges, I managed to make enough of a gap to squeeze through. The lights were on low and it was a moonless evening, so the stained-glass window was merely a swirl of greys and blacks. The private pew above was in complete darkness and I would never have known if anyone was looking down on me.

I shivered as I considered that possibility; I knew Sian couldn't be up there, though. You entered the pew from a door on the first floor and it was always locked outside of visitor hours. Even then, the public weren't meant to go in; they could only peer into the space from behind a barrier at the door. So logic told me I was alone. Shadows, imagination and pure paranoia were trying to convince me otherwise.

I tiptoed through to the vestry. The light in the meeting room was off, but Craig had left the door to his office open and a desk lamp glowed, casting shadows onto the figure sitting at the desk who looked up as I reached the door.

'Sophie, I was just trying to decide what to write in Father Craig's Christmas card.' The gold ribbon that had been tied into a bow glinted on the top of Peggy's head. She was chewing on the end of a pen, occasionally putting it to the card, and then changing her mind, giving it another chew.

'You should be at the party, Peggy, you can do this tomorrow.'

'Oh, I know, I just needed a quiet sit down and a break from the syrupy self-congratulatory performance of those three.'

'Those three?'

'Verity, Sian and Kenneth. Although Kenneth isn't so bad. You'd think the other two had just finished building the Egyptian pyramids. You're not meant to volunteer for the praise, but for the love of it; the love of this chapel and its community; for Father Craig.'

There was a seat in the corner so I sat down. Sian would have long since vanished.

'Father Craig works so hard, has from the minute he got here. He really is unlike anyone else I've met. He needs genuinely committed hard-working volunteers around him.'

'Like you?' I offered.

'I feel like I did my bit.'

'You did more than that. From everything I've heard, you were key to a lot of the trips and events. Why did you stop?'

Peggy chewed the top of her pen again. 'I didn't have much choice. The new ones were coming in with their fancy ideas, wanting to try different things. Some of them have useful skills. I know Kenneth has been helpful with the chapel finances, but you'd think that would be enough. I came back off holiday last year and Kenneth had practically moved into this office. Then Sian and Verity come trailing along behind him and that was that. They were running events and sitting on committees. And Father Craig seemed to get caught up in it all.'

Peggy's concerns didn't quite add up. 'But Harriet is still involved in most things.'

'Harriet isn't always involved. She has an opinion and makes sure everyone knows it, that's different.'

'But she helped organise the Christmas party.'

'Harriet will turn up when she feels like it and elbow her way onto committees. No one dare question her, not to her face. I'm not like that. I'm much more… respectful.'

'So you didn't stay away because you wanted to, nor because you needed to take on more cleaning shifts and earn more money?'

'Heavens, no!' she exclaimed. 'Who told you that claptrap? I wouldn't abandon Father Craig. I just… well, I do what I can.' She rested a hand on a leather notepad on his desk. It was one of the many gifts he had received over the last few weeks. My eye went back to the gold ribbon in her hair – ribbon that I recognised. The answer was staring me in the face.

'Why didn't you say the gifts were from you, Peggy? Why didn't you put a tag on them?'

She glanced up at me, a flicker of surprise on her face, but it quickly disappeared.

'It doesn't matter who they are from, just that he knows he is appreciated.'

'But they were almost every day, Peggy, does that not seem a bit excessive?'

'Nothing is too much for Father Craig,' she bit back. Her features appeared a little harder in the half light of the lamp. Her compact figure was slouched over the desk, giving her back a hunched shape. She was beginning to look goblin-like.

'Hang on!' I exclaimed. 'That means you left those cookies on my desk. Why would you leave cookies filled with winterberries for me? If I hadn't realised what they were, I could have been really sick.'

Like the clang of an enormous bell going off in my head, I realised what I'd just said.

'You left the cookies for the others that night, and put berries in their mulled wine. Why did you do it?'

There was that flicker of surprise again, but it vanished as quickly as it came.

'I helped turn a group of half-hearted, poorly led volunteers into a vibrant community – alongside Father Craig once he arrived, of course. I was the one he would listen to when he first arrived. He'd run ideas past me, he valued my opinion. Harriet has always been here, of course, but she's... well, Harriet. Not very dynamic.

'The last year has been different. They elbowed me out of the way and took over. They needed to be reminded that they didn't have control of everything. That they didn't get to make all the decisions. I'm not just some invisible cleaner that comes and goes from rooms without anyone paying them the first bit of attention. I am here, I am *still* here.'

She was right. Cleaners have one of the least glamorous, often most unpleasant jobs, get paid the least, and they quickly become invisible. Half the time when a cleaner came in, I didn't notice that they were there. They became part of the furniture, the wallpaper.

A feeling of guilt came over me when I remembered the time that a new cleaner had started work at one of my old restaurants. The woman had been emptying the bins in my office for a month before I realised it wasn't the usual person. Peggy, however, had used that anonymity to her advantage. I was almost impressed.

'You banked on them not realising you were there in order to poison them. You could come and go and they paid no attention.'

'Not quite, I don't have an invisibility cloak. There were other volunteers in the vestry before their meeting; I just hung around. I didn't have any bags with me; I didn't leave to fetch anything and return. No one paid any attention to me cleaning in the chapel or wiping the surfaces in the kitchen once the others had left. None of the four spotted me coming in while they were poring over pictures of table decorations and deciding on which tablecloths to use. No one really knew or noticed my movements. So even without a cloak, I was in effect invisible.'

She sounded so calm, like poisoning someone was just another task on the to-do list.

'And you hid everything you needed in your cleaning caddy. No one saw you carrying a bag or with bulging pockets because everything was tucked away with your cleaning products.' It was so simple.

'That caddy's been very useful. I have to admit to often having a chocolate biscuit with me when I'm cleaning in the public part of the house, or I've hidden my takeout coffee. I know it's against the rules, but I'm always careful and no one finds out.'

If she was equating sneaking a chocolate biscuit into the building with poisoning a group of people, then I doubted she was ever going to see what she'd done as wrong.

'Why did you try and poison me as well?'

'You were spending too much time trying to work it out, I just wanted you to leave it alone. There weren't many berries in your cookies, I like you.' She said it so nonchalantly. She continued to mull over the card in front of her and occasionally chew the end of the pen, not trying to run or make excuses for what she had done. I was no longer sure whether I should be impressed or terrified. There was something very cold and heartless about the blandness with which she went about describing things. As though we were both going to leave the room and never talk of it again.

'Sophie!' Craig walked in. 'Oh, Peggy, you're here. You've both missed the Duchess's speech, it was really lovely. I've come to fetch a book I promised to lend to the Duke.' He searched through the books on a shelf until he found what he was looking for, turned and glanced back and forth between the two of us.

'Is everything okay?' He seemed unsure, a little nervous. I didn't blame him; the atmosphere was distinctly odd.

'Peggy has something to tell you,' I said.

'Do I? I don't think so. We'll be back through in a moment, Father.'

'Are you kidding me? You poisoned four of the volunteers and tried to poison me, you're obsessively leaving gifts for Father Craig and you don't have anything to say?'

Craig froze. 'Peggy? Is this true?'

She looked at him. 'I do miss working with you so closely. We made such a wonderful team, don't you think? I wanted to show my appreciation for the way you've brought our community back together. I just wish some of the new members hadn't stepped on everything we'd achieved; I still had so much to give, you know.'

She smiled, but now it just looked creepy. To think I'd fallen for the salt-of-the-earth hard-working persona she had shown us all. Perhaps that was genuine and she was a female Jekyll and Hyde, with mop in one hand and poisonous berries in the other.

'Sophie?' Craig asked without looking away from Peggy. 'What do we do now?'

Peggy started to write on the Christmas card, having apparently found the perfect words in this utterly bizarre moment.

'I'll stay here and call the police. You go back to the party and pretend everything is okay, but do have a quiet word with the Duke and Duchess. I'm sure DS Harnby can handle this very discreetly.'

'Will you be okay on your own?' he asked with concern. I looked at Peggy; it was a risk I was willing to take. By the looks of things, she needed help, not arresting, and I really didn't think any harm would come to me.

'I'll be fine.'

'ny idea where Sian went?' I asked Craig as we watched Peggy being led down the lane by Joe, DS Harnby holding the back door of the police car open for them.

'No idea,' Craig answered. 'But based on what you've just told me, I would imagine that she might have realised you were filling Kenneth in and she's skulked off home. But if Peggy was the one who poisoned them, Sian doesn't seem to be a threat. It would be interesting to see what she's playing at, why she's concealed her identity.'

'Let's hope she's *not* planning anything. This should put her off if she is,' I said, hopefully. Harnby closed the door of the car once Peggy was safely inside and walked back towards me.

'I'll leave you and the sergeant to exchange notes. I need to help tidy up the party.' Craig went back inside.

'What gave her away?' Harnby asked.

'She was invisible,' I said. 'When she was telling me about the changes over the last year, she was basically saying she felt unseen. Craig's attention had gone elsewhere and new volunteers had taken her place as the hub of a lot of the projects and activity planning. Add to that a job where she often really *is* unseen and you've got the perfect way of hiding in plain sight.

'The other thing was a comment that Chelsea made. She said the poisoning sounded like teenagers who were playing up and doing stupid stuff to get attention. I realised Peggy didn't want to be invisible, she *was* trying to get attention. I'd been too focused on more obvious reasons for wanting to poison someone, like an act of revenge for a particular event, but this was a gradual thing.'

Harnby nodded thoughtfully. 'We did pretty much the same thing, made the same mistake,' she admitted, a little more quickly than I'd expected. 'We knew about Kenneth managing to make himself enemies through work, and when we interviewed Sian, she told us about her brother and using a different name. But there was absolutely no evidence that tied her to the poisoning. It was a very frustrating yet tantalising dead end.'

'When did you find out about that?'

'Last week.'

'Great. So I've been digging around, trying to find out motives for murder, and you knew all about Sian and ruled her out ages ago?'

'We are the police, Sophie, we're able to carry out our own investigations, and we're under no obligation to tell you anything.'

I knew she was right, but still, it rankled.

'So what was she up to if she didn't poison anyone, and yet she had reason to be mad at Kenneth? Why did she use a false name? I'm confused.'

'It seemed she did actually plan on getting her own back on Kenneth; he might have had a narrow escape. When he was first working with her brother, Kenneth had mentioned that he went to a wine club. When it all went sour, Sian joined the club under a variation of her name. She befriended Kenneth, made up a few things about her background and work history. After becoming friends with her, he invited her to come along to the chapel. Only problem was she started to like him. Claimed that she grew really close to him, but could never find a good time to explain what her real name was, so she continued the charade.'

'So she fell in love with the target of her revenge, how very Shakespearean.'

'You make it sound more dramatic than it was.'

'Still, you could have dropped a few clues here or there. I might have figured out it was Peggy sooner if I hadn't been distracted by Sian. I tell you what I've found out.'

Harnby threw her head back and laughed.

'You do not! Not all the time, anyway. And often when you do, it's because you've waited until you've seen me, rather than calling me the minute you find something. Case in point, you didn't tell me about Sian's surname when you first found out, regardless of whether or not I already knew.'

A sheepish smile turned up one corner of my mouth. 'Okay, point taken.'

'It was easier when Joe was hanging around your café. He often came back to the station with some little snippet or other. Can't you two...'

'Can't we two what?'

'Get back to doing whatever it was you were doing. Not quite dating, but...'

'Not dating at all. At. All. We were just friends, still are. Only now he's seeing Ellie so he's busy... well, you know.' I let my sentence trail off into an awkward silence; I was sure that Harnby didn't want to be discussing the private life of one of her team.

A gust of wind sent our hair swirling and we both put our hands to our heads. It was dark and cold; I knew that rain was forecast to return.

Harnby turned towards the unmarked police car that remained in the lane.

'Good luck tomorrow. I won't be able to make it, but I'm sure you'll be great.'

Dammit! I'd managed to forget all about the staff Christmas service. I groaned and ran back inside out of the cold.

Pumpkin ran down the hallway towards me, head-butting my legs, and I quickly put my bag on the floor so I could pick her up. She carefully chose the moments she wanted to be affectionate, and I always tried to make the most of them. I kissed the top of her head as she nuzzled into my neck.

There was a bonus to having a fat... sorry, *large-boned* cat: she was solid in my arms, which made for really good cuddles. I carried her through to the kitchen where she jumped out of my arms and alternated between rubbing against the furniture and my legs. She was a true moggy, no pure-bred genes in her anywhere, and yet her tabby markings were beautifully symmetrical. The stripes on her face looked like face paint carefully applied in front of a mirror. The stripes on her legs matched. She was moody and capable of giving me the best sly eye in the business, but catch her on a good day and in the right light, and she was the most loving, beautiful creature. This was one of the rare nights when she had decided I was alright.

I'd eaten enough of the party buffet to keep me going until the morning, so I opted for a drink that I save for when I'm feeling at my most lazy: a can of gin and tonic. Some days I'll tell you they are the ultimate sacrilege, but on a night like tonight, they are pretty much all I can manage to conjure up.

With Pumpkin fed and my drink rattling around in a glass with a handful of ice cubes, I made my way to the sofa and got comfortable. As I started to lie down, I remembered something I wanted to talk to Harnby about and sat back up. With the sound of Jess's tongue piercing rattling against her teeth in my mind, I picked up my phone and dialled.

'Hello there, stranger, thank you for once again beating us to it.' Curse it, I'd dialled Joe's number rather than Harnby's. Force of habit, I guess. 'You really are going to give us a bad name.'

'I'm sure you can do that all by yourself,' I tossed back, hoping he knew I was kidding. 'I'm sorry to disturb you, I know you're dealing with Peggy, but do you have a minute?'

'Sure. Harnby's with Peggy, I'm just sifting through paperwork. How can I help you keep our clear up rates high?'

'Dwin Lee.'

'What about him?'

'Can you have someone check the information on his teeth?'

'Errr, I guess so. Are you worried he wasn't flossing?'

'Not exactly. I might be way off the mark, but I'm just wondering about something and I need to put my mind at rest.'

I could picture Joe scribbling a note down in a pad, and then leaning back in his chair, probably putting his feet on the desk.

'You're not going to tell me what this is about?'

'Not yet. Give me a call when you've got it and I'll tell you what I'm thinking.'

'Okay, Sherlock, your wish appears to be my command. Speak later.' He hung up and I smiled. It was nice to talk to him, no matter how briefly.

I rested my head back on the cushion and let my smile wane. I had misread Peggy since the day I started at Charleton House. I didn't know her very well, but she had been cheerful and encouraging when I'd arrived. She always had a smile, no matter what the time of day, and I'd admired her positivity. It was a tough lesson in how wrong you can be about someone.

Then I started to wonder about Dwin, George, Catherine, William and Mary. A cast of characters I could never meet, who I was judging on a very small amount of their own words or the opinions of others. Was I wrong there, too? Was Mary just a sweet, misguided young thing who liked a bit of gossip and made a mistake she regretted for the rest of her days? Was George a confused young man who, in a world of status, struggled being the youngest son with no particular role within the family? How about William? A widowed business owner who wasn't coping with the job of running a pub while lovingly supporting a daughter without a mother in her life?

I really hoped that we were getting a true picture. We'd never know for sure. None of them were the kind of people to leave behind endless trails of evidence, or have works written about them at the time. They weren't kings or queens, diarists, or celebrities of any kind, not even George. Just like most of us, I suppose. But they weren't forgotten, not now. I'd do my best for them and get as close as I could to the truth.

CHAPTER 30

The chapel was filling up. The staff Christmas service was always very popular and there was usually an overflow of people standing at the back; this year was going to be no different.

A weak, watery sun did its best to spread the colours of the stained glass around the church. The bows at the ends of the pews had been straightened up and the bright new kneelers were back in place. Two volunteers stood at the door, welcoming everyone as they entered. Harriet, in a brown blazer and a red silk scarf knotted at her neck, gave me the first smile I had ever seen cross her face. She seemed to struggle to make it appear, but in her eyes it was firm and fast and genuine. I smiled back. I didn't know if Peggy's arrest had become common knowledge. I guessed not, but it wouldn't be long before the gossip spread around the house like wildfire, and somehow, I had no idea how, Harriet would probably be the first to know.

Kenneth and Verity had taken their places in a pew halfway down the aisle. Sian was tucked away in a corner towards the back. I saw Joyce's hair before I saw the rest of her. She was down at the front and had saved me a seat.

'Sophie!' she said, sounding a little exasperated. 'I know we're in a church, but it's not a funeral.' I'd opted for my usual black suit.

'But what about the shirt? Red is festive.'

'Yes, I suppose. Come on.' She shuffled up to make room for me and I gave her outfit the once over. She had on a beautiful cream mohair sweater with a cowl neck. Over it she wore a simple long gold chain with a beautiful little Christmas tree hanging pendant. I looked closely and saw that the baubles on the tree were tiny pearls. Her brown suede skirt and matching shoes completed an elegant outfit. The skirt was still tight enough that I could tell the style of knickers she was wearing, but that was only to be expected. Her straw blonde hair was piled on her head in her signature style, but even the wispy bits that hung down seemed more consciously placed than usual.

I often joked about Joyce's wardrobe; there was nothing to joke about today. She looked stunning, while I felt like I'd dragged myself out of a hot and steamy kitchen in a suit I'd worn all week. It wasn't true. The suit was just back from the dry cleaners, and I'd chosen my red shirt, with a delicate black polka dot pattern, carefully, but next to Joyce I felt frumpy. Perhaps I should let her take me shopping for clothes after all. The thought had always terrified me, but looking at her now, I had to concede that perhaps it wouldn't be so bad.

As the final people filed in with the organ playing softly in the background, I could feel my hands becoming increasingly hot and sticky. I couldn't stop my right knee from bobbing up and down. Joyce reached across and grabbed hold of my knee force-fully and held it in place.

'You'll be fine!' she declared through gritted teeth. It was an order, not an encouragement.

The service was a shorter version of the Nine Lessons and Carols. After 'O Little Town of Bethlehem' in which a few creaky old sopranos pulled out all the stops remembering the descants, and a rousing rendition of 'O Come All Ye Faithful', it was my turn. As the final few bars were played, I shuffled my papers and took a few deep breaths. I'd stopped sweating, but I wasn't convinced I could stop my hands shaking, or even get the words out at all.

I was about to stand up when I felt my phone vibrate in my jacket pocket. Thankfully I'd remembered to put it in silent mode. I didn't have time to look at it in detail, but a quick glance told me it was from Joe and the message started with *'Well, they were all his own teeth...'* I'd have to look at it properly when I had finished humiliating myself. First, I had some shepherds and their flocks to attend to.

I had to clear my throat multiple times before I started, and I was convinced I'd sound as if I'd just swallowed a sack of sand. But after a while, I managed to get going, and strangely, I started to enjoy myself. The splendid chapel, the feeling of being part of a special moment, of a community, worked its magic. As I started to feel confident enough about the next couple of sentences, I would glance up and check out the sea of faces. So many of them familiar, most of them friendly (Sian looked like she wanted to stab me at the first available opportunity and Harriet had gone back to sucking a lemon), willing me on, or so it seemed. Instead of worrying about faith and what I believed or not, I chose to think of myself as a storyteller. The words were familiar and strangely comforting, and as a result, in what felt like no time at all, I was stepping down from the pulpit and making my way back to the pew.

As I sat down, Joyce slapped my thigh so hard it stung. She was grinning.

'Told you! You were great,' she whispered loudly. A hand appeared from behind and gave my shoulder a squeeze; someone across the aisle leaned into my eye line and gave me a thumbs up.

I'd done it.

I didn't really hear the reading from St John's Gospel that

Craig finished with; I was too relieved and spent my time admiring the Nativity scene in the far corner and wondering if my team had the café all ready for later. Once the service was over, I floated down the aisle. The expression about a weight lifting from your shoulders had never felt more apt.

CHAPTER 31

*I*t was tradition, after the staff service, for everyone in attendance to enjoy a glass of spiced cider and a mince pie. As the house was closed to the public by the time the service had ended, it was agreed that we would hold the gathering in the Library Café, and I tried to get ahead of the crowd to have a quick glance at the place before everyone arrived. I was only seconds ahead, but needn't have worried.

Chelsea and Tina had decorated the tables with sprigs of holly and fir cones. There wasn't a winterberry in sight. Gregg had laid out plates with carefully balanced piles of mince pies, and the shiny copper pot that had been used in the Garden Café last night was back in pride of place. He stood behind it, ladling out glasses of steaming hot cider as the crowd arrived. Gregg had actually worked with a wassail recipe and tried to make it as authentic as possible. It was a hot spiced cider with sugar, cinnamon, ginger and nutmeg added which used to be served in a wooden wassail bowl, but we hadn't gone that far.

As the noise levels rose and the café became so full that people had to squeeze past one another, I caught Mark's eye and waved at him. I hadn't been able to see him in the chapel, but I knew he'd have been there. He grinned and waved back. It took another frantic wave from me for him to realise I actually wanted him to join me in the kitchen. I did the same to Joyce and she leapt at a chance to escape the attention of a member of the Charleton House Trust, the charitable branch of the business.

'Hot, sweaty handshake and bad breath,' she grumbled as she reached me. 'Thanks for the rescue. I was waiting for him to ask me on a date.'

'You're full of yourself,' said Mark, arriving just in time to catch her last comment. Joyce ignored him. 'How can we help?'

I led them through to my office, which has been referred to variously as a matchbox, a coffin, and less spacious than one of our ovens – and in the summer, hotter, while in winter, it requires me to work with a blanket over my knees if I'm not going to freeze to death. Offices in historic houses are invariably unusual and have a thermostat all of their own, and my tiny hole has just enough space for my chair to turn round in.

Joyce immediately took the chair. With her legs crossed, her skirt practically vanished up to her armpits; I tried not to stare. Mark stood in a corner and begged Joyce not to swivel the chair round for fear she would kneecap him, and I sat on the edge of my desk.

'I know who killed Dwin. Or at least, I'm very, very sure I know who killed Dwin. I want to run my theory past you before I tell Harnby, and definitely before I tell the Duke and Duchess.'

Joyce smiled like a proud parent. 'I knew you'd figure it out.'

Mark looked curious. 'Go on. I have a theory of my own, but let's see if they match.'

'Does this mean there was killer in the Fitzwilliam-Scott family?' Joyce asked, unable to wait for me to start explaining the way I'd put all the jigsaw pieces together. There was a knock on the door and Chelsea stuck her head in.

'Oh, sorry.'

'It's okay, do you need something?'

'Yes, Tina's burnt her hand. She's okay, but we could do with some help. Coming...' she shouted over her shoulder. I'd heard Gregg come into the kitchen behind her and say they needed more mince pies. 'Sorry,' she added before shutting the door behind her.

'Sorry, folks,' I said, 'you're going to have to wait. But I do want to make sure you don't think I'm crazy.'

'That ship has sailed,' said Mark as he waited for Joyce and me to get out of the way.

'This is worse than being told I can't open my Christmas presents until after we've all eaten breakfast,' Joyce declared as she walked past me. 'I didn't realise you were quite so mean, dangling it in front of us like that before whipping it away.'

'Hey, it's not my fault. I'll go and have stern words with Tina: "How dare you hurt yourself! It was inconsiderate, go and apologise to Joyce right now".'

'Sounds reasonable to me,' were the last words Joyce said to me as she walked out.

After checking on Tina, who was standing at the sink running cold water over her hand, I picked up a platter of mince pies and walked into the throng. I didn't get very far before I came face to face with Harriet. Her glass of wassail was empty and she had a glow on her cheeks.

'Sophie, a minute of your time, please.' I didn't have any choice. I handed the mince pies to Mark and told him to circulate, then followed Harriet into a corner.

'Sophie, I will not entertain rule breaking in the chapel. Food, drink, excessive noise, treating it like a public house. I will still stop you if you enter with a drink, and I don't care if it is for Craig; you must go round the back and use the appropriate entrance into the vestry. But despite your determination to bend the rules, I do acknowledge, you're a good person.'

Gregg walked past with a jug of wassail and Harriet stuck her glass out in front of him so he could refill it. I wondered how many of those she'd had. Gregg glanced at me with a look of comical surprise on his face as he walked away.

'I, along with everyone else I imagine, assumed those berries were for me. I have no idea why, but you didn't seem to hold the same view and didn't let the matter rest.' She took a big swig of her steaming drink. 'I have something for you. Follow me.'

Harriet led the way out of the café, breaking every rule in the book by taking her glass with her. I thought she hiccupped, but I couldn't swear to it. She marched out into the cold and along the back lane. I had no idea where we were going, but wished I'd been allowed to fetch my coat. I had to do a half run, half walk to keep up with Harriet; her age and stature were deceptive. She was like a little terrier.

Security had already seen us coming and raised the barrier, probably realising that was safer than expecting us to navigate the pedestrian gate as Harriet showed no signs of slowing down. I waved at the security officer and ensured we had eye contact; I wanted to be certain he had clearly seen me leave with Harriet, just in case I disappeared and no one could find my body.

She only slowed as we neared her car. She tipped her head back, and after finishing every last drop, she put the glass on the roof of the car. Still, she didn't say a word. Opening the boot, she reached for something that had been wrapped in tissue paper.

'I realise you might be a little wary of Christmas gifts right now, but this is for you.' It sounded like an instruction rather than a sentimental offering.

I stood next to her and rested the gift on the boot of the car as I unwrapped it. As the tissue paper fell away, I found myself looking at the most beautiful painting of Charleton House. The sunlight glinted off the gilded window frames on a bright autumnal morning. Mist still lay low upon the grass, and to one side, in the foreground, was a magnificent stag, looking at the scene with me. I knew of course that this was the work of Harriet herself.

There was no way of fighting the tears that hovered in the corners of my eyes. Fortunately they clung on and stayed there, but Harriet seemed to spot them.

'Yes, well, I hope you like it.' She stepped back, making it clear that our moment was over. I wrapped the painting back up and tucked it safely under my arm.

'Thank you, this will take pride of place at home. Harriet, I know...'

'Yes, that's fine,' she butted in awkwardly, slamming the boot of the car and firmly ending any conversation.

'Your glass...'

'I know! What do you take me for?' She snatched her empty glass off the roof of the car and we retraced our steps back to the café, only this time we walked side by side.

CHAPTER 32

$\mathcal{M}$y hands were shaking again. This time, I wasn't about to give a public performance; at least, not with quite so large an audience.

After the café had been cleared of staff and I'd eaten a few mince pies too many, I'd had the opportunity to talk to Mark and Joyce. They had concluded that I wasn't entirely out of my mind and it was worth calling DS Harnby. With all my evidence laid before her, she'd also decided that I hadn't overdone the wassail and felt it was indeed time we went and talked to the Duke and Duchess.

So here I was with Mark beside me, taking a seat in their elegant dining room with its shimmering gold and white wallpaper, surrounded by paintings of the estate over the centuries, to lay out what evidence I had, my notes in front of me to help me fill in the gaps. I hadn't been this nervous since I'd arrived at Charleton House for my job interview. But it wasn't just that I was worried about their reaction. It was important to me; I felt that I was doing this for Dwin and Catherine.

I could picture Catherine quite easily, having seen her photograph. This wasn't the case with Dwin, but I had created an image of him. A kindly looking old man with white hair and a white beard that framed his face, and a watery twinkle in his eye. I was probably romanticising him, but it had given me something to hold on to as I had tried to wrap my brain around the clues.

With everyone seated, I looked around at the expectant faces, wondering where to start.

'Why don't you talk us through your thinking, show us how you ended up where you have?' I should have known that the Duchess would be the one to try and put me at my ease, giving me a framework for explaining things.

'Okay. Mark, please join in; you did just as much of the work.'

He nodded. I took a deep breath.

'We're as sure as we can be that the skeleton in the Black Swan is that of Edwin Lee, or Dwin. Everything we know about him points to him having been a kindly old man who didn't do anyone any harm. As far as anyone knew at the time, he'd gone missing and was never seen again. Fortunately for his killer, he wasn't someone considered to be of any great significance, otherwise more effort might have been made to find him.

'Based on the name of her child, I believe Catherine struck up a friendship with him and they became close – you don't name your child after someone unless they are important to you. I imagine Dwin as being an advisor of sorts, a father figure in the way her real father wasn't.

'Someone else Catherine confided in was Mary Ollerenshaw. She worked here at Charleton as a maid – her diary gives us a fascinating insight into life below stairs at that time. Luckily for us, she also recorded gossip and the ins and outs of her friendship with Catherine; she was a pretty typical teenager in that way.

'It's through Mary that we learn Catherine had an admirer. She was a beautiful young woman, so I imagine she had many, but this one seemed to have charmed her. He was a wealthy gentleman who had promised to support her and her father.'

'Pops was hugely in debt,' Mark joined in. 'We have receipts from the brewery, and he eventually lost the business because of his illegal attempts to make money.'

He nodded for me to continue.

'I'm afraid this is where your family comes in, and it's not too flattering.'

The Duke waved my concern away. 'I always knew if it involved George, it wasn't going to be a story about Prince Charming.'

'He had rather a reputation, liked the ladies.'

'That's an understatement!' laughed the Duke. 'Sorry, do go on.'

'Included in his tastes were some of the servants. It seemed he wasn't too concerned about social status if the fancy took him, and he had the occasional liaison with a member of staff. Young Mary Ollerenshaw wasn't amongst those, but we can be sure she would have liked to have been, although she ultimately escaped a broken heart by going under George's radar.

'That's the other thing that convinced me George was Catherine's admirer. Mary fell out with her friend; she was furious at her, and the one thing that would have caused such emotion was her feelings for George, who she was madly in love with. So much so it cost Mary her job. Her anger was pure jealousy.

'I'm certain that Catherine caught his eye, and so the admirer who was going to rescue her father's business was George. In reality, he had no such plans. He wanted to bed Catherine like he had all the women before her and, attempting to charm his way into her affection, he would say whatever he thought she wanted to hear. We know how frustrated his parents were becoming by his unwillingness to settle down; it would have taken a personality transplant for him to change that attitude over the daughter of a debt-ridden landlord.'

I pushed the practice letter that William had been working on towards Mark. It was his turn. I took a glass of water as he talked.

'Around this time, there are references to a project or some sort of business opportunity that William was engaging in that would enable him to pay off those debts. As you know, Duke, it wasn't uncommon for your family members to invest in local businesses, as you yourself do to this day. However, that wasn't in character for George. He wasn't a... shall we say "charitable chap"? If you think about it, Catherine reports that her admirer is going to pay off the family debts, and we think that admirer is George. William is talking about being able to pay his creditors, and yet it doesn't happen. Something is stopping it.'

'It's an awful thing to say—' I looked at the Duchess for reassurance and she tilted her head, ready to hear more '—but I think that George wanted something in return. First, he wanted Catherine. Not to marry, not really, but he had his eye on her. I also think that Dwin was advising Catherine against getting involved. He was a local man, he would have known all the ins and outs of village life, and he would have known George's reputation. He liked Catherine and wouldn't have wanted her to be taken advantage of. If George had convinced William that he would pay off his debts, and more, if he could have his daughter's hand in marriage, then William would have been encouraging her, none the wiser – or not caring – whether or not George was genuine.'

'So,' added Mark, 'Dwin was the block that was in the way of this financial relationship taking place.'

'It's awful to think of a young woman being considered part of a financial arrangement, just awful.' The Duchess sounded genuinely horrified. I agreed.

'The question is, how is that block removed? At the time, there was a man called Michael Hall working here, too. He was involved in a fight and later hung for murder. There's every chance that George met him on the estate and knew his reputation. So, one thought was that George got Michael to get rid of

Dwin. The brawl that took place at the Plough on the day of Dwin's disappearance would have been the perfect distraction.'

'So George paid for a man to be killed?' The Duke was shocked. 'Although I suppose that was better than what I thought you were going to say.'

'That George did it himself?' I asked. 'No, it crossed my mind, too, but then we realised that George was in London and we heard about Michael who was certainly capable of murder. But that's not what I think happened. If George had paid Michael, then he wouldn't want there to be any evidence that he was involved. He wouldn't have told William. Dwin would have just vanished, leaving Catherine to be convinced by George and her father. Problem solved. But only a matter of days after Dwin vanished, William wrote a note to George.'

I pulled out the note I had found amongst Mary's stolen items, the note that told George there was no longer anything in the way of their plans going ahead, placing it next to the letter William had been practising. The handwriting was exactly the same.

'How did William know there was no longer a problem? How did he know that Dwin wasn't going to come back into the pub later that week and continue to try and protect Catherine?' I looked around the table at the faces that were staring back, mouths slightly open.

The Duke was the one to speak. 'Because he killed him.'

I nodded slowly. 'Yes, that's what I think happened. In one of the photos of William that we've seen, he has a pipe in his pocket. Clay pipes were incredibly common in those days so I thought nothing of it when one was found with Dwin. But I asked for his dental records to be checked. Even now, you'd have been able to see some discolouration if he was a regular smoker, and there's also a strong chance that the pipe would have worn his teeth. As I did my research on this, I saw a photo of a set of teeth that had a perfect pipe-shaped groove in the front, and that skeleton was older than Dwin's. His teeth have no such mark. He wasn't a pipe smoker.

'I suspect the pipe fell out of William's pocket when he was hiding Dwin's body and he never noticed. I realise that many of the men who went to the pub would have smoked, but William had a reason to get rid of Dwin. He had the opportunity when the brawl took place, and he'd kicked everyone out, to kill Dwin. I imagine Dwin would have returned pretty quickly to check that Catherine was okay. William would also have had quite a bit of time to hide the body after everything had calmed down.

'He then sends this note to George, who pays off some of the debts as promised to attempt to look honourable. Mark saw evidence of the payments here in the stores. We thought the payments to breweries were for parties here, but the timing is too much of a coincidence. Catherine then no longer had anyone to dissuade her from a relationship with George. Her father was no doubt encouraging it, especially having had some of his debts paid, and she was a good daughter. She wanted to help her father, help get him out of debt. Roughly nine months later, she gives birth.'

The Duchess let out a loud sigh. 'While George gets married and seemingly enters respectable society.' She looked over at her husband. 'Bloody men!'

'Why are you looking at me?' he asked, shocked innocence in his voice. 'I don't even forget your birthday. Seriously, though, it's dreadful. What happened to Catherine and the child?'

I paused, fighting a lump in my throat. 'She died, either during or not long after the birth. The son also died.' The Duke dropped his head. 'The boy was named Edwin Lee, after the man who had tried to protect his mother. If it's any consolation, we suspect George's parents found out about their son's behaviour towards poor Catherine and it was they who paid for her burial, and for the headstone to commemorate her and her son.'

We sat in silence for a few minutes.

'Are you sure about all this?' the Duke asked me. 'I don't mean to doubt you, I'm just…'

'It's okay. I understand. Am I 100% certain? No, that's impossible. But am I as certain as I can be, based on the evidence I've seen? Yes. I'm certain enough to sit here and tell you that I believe William Austin killed Edwin Lee.'

'Then that's good enough for me, Sophie. Thank you, both of you.'

The Duchess took hold of her husband's hand and turned to face me. 'What's going to happen to Dwin's remains?'

'I was hoping… we were going to ask how you felt about burying him at St Anne's? There's room next to Catherine and her son.'

'Perfect!' declared the Duke loudly. His outburst broke the atmosphere of sadness that had firmly settled around us. 'I'll tell Father Craig to organise it.'

CHAPTER 33

*C*raig managed to arrange things for Dwin's burial quite quickly.

'I don't want him to get forgotten again, he deserves our attention, now,' was how Craig had described it. And so, two days before Christmas, a small group of us gathered at St Anne's church.

The Duke and Duchess led us all to the graveside. Joyce, in a long black coat, had opted against a celebration of life via her wardrobe, but still chose to teeter carefully across the grass in unnervingly high heels. Fortunately, the day had opened with a hard frost which likely prevented her sinking into the ground a couple of inches.

Chelsea had asked for the morning off so she could attend and stood with Steve and Rosemary. As the landlord and land-lady had discussed the planned service with Craig in the pub, they'd spoken of Dwin as if he was family.

As I looped my arm through Mark's, hoping his body heat would help keep me warm in the morning chill, I looked at the gravestone of Catherine and the younger Dwin. It was only right that the child's namesake would now lie next to them. He had, after all, been their protector in life. In the short service, Craig had entrusted Dwin to the care of God, and briefly said a prayer for mercy on William Austin, although he didn't mention him by name. Any sadness I felt had largely gone; instead, everything felt so incredibly 'right', like for once a part of life had been tied up neatly.

We left the graveyard quietly, each in our own thoughts. We had a normal day of work ahead of us, but I was sure we would all find our thoughts turning to Dwin throughout.

'See you later?' asked Craig as Mark and I walked through the gate.

'Of course,' I replied, hugging him. Joyce was unlocking her car.

'Come on, you two, get in. We still have a house full of bloody visitors to tend to. Let's see how many of them can find something petty to whinge about today.'

'Thanks, but I'm going to walk,' I called.

'Me too,' Mark said, waving. 'Why don't you join us? We can drop you off to pick up your car later.'

'Have you seen my shoes, Mark Boxer? You must be mad if you think I'm going to traipse through some muddy fields full of dead plants and slimy rocks and ruin these. They're a work of art.'

'Muddy fields?' echoed the Duchess. 'Do you mean my beautifully laid out gardens that have been lovingly tended throughout the year?' She raised an eyebrow at Joyce.

'Yes, I mean... of course... they're clearly going to look fabulous in the... such hard work.'

The Duchess laughed. 'Don't worry, Joyce. Although I will drag you out into my muddy fields next year so you can give me a hand.'

'Thank you. That sounds... I'll, er, see you later.' With that, Joyce ducked into her car and drove off, eyes firmly ahead. I'd never seen her flustered; it was rather fun.

'Come on, Sherlock,' Mark said as he tugged at my arm, 'you deserve a coffee.'

After such a poignant start to the day, the rest of it had become a blur of coffee and cake as visitors were swept up in the Christmas spirit that practically oozed from every room in the house. I'd remained busy enough not to dwell too much on recent events, but I was getting tired and ready to wind down and start enjoying my own Christmas.

Once we'd finished for the day, Mark and I had driven to the Black Swan where we knew the others were waiting for us. A text message from Joyce that declared '*We're in Sophie's* other *office*' didn't take much deciphering. It had been a long day and my emotions had zipped from one end of the spectrum to the other. A wall of heat from the log fire hit me as I entered the pub and my glasses immediately steamed up. I wiped them on the hem of my skirt.

Once I could see clearly again, DS Harnby handed me a drink.

'Steve says this is your usual, I made it a double.'

'Thank you, detective...'

'Call me Colette – for this evening, anyway.'

I thanked her again and took a very long drink of the gin and tonic.

'Soph... oh, you've got one. I just ordered you a gin.'

'Thanks, Father, you can start lining them up for me.'

The rest of our group had gathered at the end of the bar next to a Christmas tree. I wondered how long it would be before one of us knocked it over as I slotted myself in next to Joyce, who had a pair of large plastic snowmen hanging from her ears. On each one, a scarf was formed by a line of flashing red lights.

'Are you going to take *any* time off?' Harnby asked me.

'Only Christmas Day, we're back open on Boxing Day.'

'I meant from solving my cases for me. Only I'm wondering if

I can book a couple of weeks off in the New Year and I figured you could cover my job for me.' There was amusement in her eyes.

'Yes, she could,' interjected Joyce, 'whilst still keeping her own teams going as well. She's quite remarkable, this one.'

'I don't dispute that,' said Harnby.

I turned and tapped Bill on the shoulder as Harnby reached across to examine Joyce's earrings. He was leaning on the bar and looking intently at a piece of paper with Mark.

'Hey, Sophie, we're just planning the menu for Christmas Day. Mum has been hassling me to finalise the shopping list.'

Mark turned, a pained expression on his face. 'We're going to need a truck, multiple trucks. In fact, just get all the supermarket deliveries diverted to our house.'

'It's a big event, then?' Joyce asked. Mark rolled his eyes.

'Huge. Both halves of Bill's family come. It's like trying to plan a military operation.'

Bill and Joe's mother had remarried before Joe came along, which explained the different surnames. Their mother had stayed friends with her first husband, Bill's dad, and everyone came together on Christmas Day, birthdays and the occasional holiday. It sounded like a lot of fun, and a lot of hard work.

I watched as Steve came along the bar and spoke to Mark. I couldn't hear the conversation, but Mark looked surprised and turned to stare at me, grinning. I moved in next to him.

'What am I missing, chaps?'

'Steve here is buying all our drinks.'

'Really? Thank you, Steve, but why?'

'It's thanks to you two that we could attach a name to those bones and give him a decent burial. It's the least I can do.'

As Steve talked, I glanced down the bar.

'Where's the old guy gone?' I asked, pointing at the stool that had been taken up by him each time we'd been in recently.

'Santa? That's what the staff have taken to calling him 'cos of his beard, but not to 'is face, like. No idea. He hasn't been in today. I was wondering if I should be worried.'

I was distracted by the smell of a musky perfume and Joyce's voice in my ear.

'Don't look now, but...'

'Joyce, just spit it out. Joe's here with Ellie. Am I right?'

'Yes, is that okay?'

'Of course it's okay. It's a pub, they can go anywhere they want. It's all *fine*.' I turned and gave Ellie the biggest smile I could without looking like a clown. If she and Joe were serious, we were going to see a lot more of her, and I wanted her to feel welcome. She smiled back and I was sure I saw her visibly relax.

'Have you decided what to do about that card from your ex?' Joyce asked quietly, keeping the theme of romantic entanglements alive.

'I have. It was nice of him to send it, and I'm going to work on the basis that that's all it was, a nice gesture. But he's a part of my past. I'm not going to stew over him, I'm not going to stress about possible motives and I'm not going to try and get back in touch. The card is on display with all the others on my windowsill and that's as far as it goes. All of you, this place, Derbyshire – that's my life now, and he's not a part of it.'

'Good girl.' She toasted me with her glass and drained the rest of her prosecco. 'Well, speaking of men, I need to love you and leave you. I have a date.' She gathered up her coat and wrapped a long scarf around her neck.

'Really? Who's the victim... I mean, lucky fella?'

She gave me a mock glare before letting her smile return.

'Eric, the last landlord of this place. After we interviewed him, he gave me a call and asked me out. I decided it was worth it for old times' sake, we always had a laugh.'

She kissed me on the cheek, shouted goodbye at everyone else and disappeared into the night. I was about to head over and say hello to Joe and Ellie when Rosemary leaned across the bar and tugged on my shirtsleeve.

'Sophie, I found this and thought you might want to take a look. I don't know if it's any use now, but I was doing another search of the attic in case I'd missed anything, and... well, take a look.'

She handed me a brown envelope. Inside was one black-and-white photo. It was similar to those we'd seen earlier and I guessed it was taken at the same time.

With his back against the brick wall of the pub, the doorway just in shot to his right, stood an elderly gentleman. He stood a little awkwardly, like he couldn't get one leg to straighten up. His well-worn jacket looked a size too big for him, the elbows of the sleeves were threadbare and his shirt showed through. He had kind eyes and a warm, nervous smile shone through the white hairs of his beard and moustache.

I held my breath as I took in the photo of the man who could only have been Edwin Lee. Slowly, I raised my head and looked down towards the end of the bar. The stool remained empty and I doubted I'd see the old man again. He no longer had incomplete business to attend to here at the Black Swan, or the Plough, as he probably remembered it.

'Happy Christmas, Dwin,' I whispered, raising my glass. 'Happy Christmas.'

READ THE FIRST CHARLETON HOUSE MYSTERY

Building a relationship with my readers is one of the best things about writing. I occasionally send newsletters with details on new releases, special offers, interviews and articles relating to The Charleton House Mysteries.

Sign up to my mailing list and you'll also receive the very first Charleton House Mystery, *A Stately Murder*.

Head to my website for your free copy and find out what happens when Sophie stumbles across the victim of the first murder Charleton House has ever known.

www.katepadams.com

ABOUT THE AUTHOR

After 25 years working in some of England's finest buildings, Kate P. Adams has turned to murder.

Kate grew up in Derbyshire, the setting for the Charleton House Mysteries, and went on to work in theatres around the country, the Natural History Museum - London, the University of Oxford and Hampton Court Palace. Every day she explored darkened corridors and rooms full of history behind doors the public never get to enter. Kate spent years in these beautiful buildings listening to fantastic tales, wondering where the bodies were hidden, and hoping that she'd run into a ghost or two.

Kate has an unhealthy obsession with finding the perfect cup of coffee, enjoys a gin and tonic, and is managed by Pumpkin, a domineering tabby cat who is a little on the large side. Now that she lives in the USA, writing the Charleton House Mysteries allows Kate to go home to be her beloved Derbyshire everyday, in her head at least.

ACKNOWLEDGEMENTS

Thank you to my beta readers Lynne McCormack, Helen McNally, Eileen Minchin, and Rosanna Summers. Your honesty and insightful comments help make my books so much better than they would otherwise be.

Many thanks to my advance readers, your support and feedback means a great deal to me. Thank you to all my readers. I love hearing from you.

Thank you to Dr Heather Bonney, Principal Curator, Human Remains and Anthropology at the Natural History Museum London, who provided me with fascinating facts about skeletons and gave me some great ideas to work with: Martyn Cornell, whose beer-related knowledge was invaluable: Joanne Hancox gave me insight into the world of finance: Kerren Harris, whose conservation expertise helps me protect Charleton House and its contents: Susie Stokoe, Textile Department Supervisor at Chatsworth House, shared their approach to Christmas and conservation. Rev'd Canon Anthony Howe, Susanne Mitchell and Debbie Young all gave me helpful insights into the subject of faith.

I'm extremely grateful to Richard Mason, my police advisor who guides me on procedure and makes sure I am, largely, within the law. When I break the rules, that's all me!

My wonderful editor Alison Jack, and Julia Gibbs, my eagle-eyed proofreader. Both are worth their weight in gold.

Thank you to Susan Stark; without her support my imaginary friends would have to remain in my head.